Matty's Dread: A Trekker's Hegira

Merry Christmas !
David 2018
from your garage sale
buddy
Gail L. Harwood -

By Gail L. Harwood

 First edition 2016

ISBN 978-0-9950812-0-8

Amazon.com

Contact the author at: gharwood@shaw.ca

or Gail Harwood on Facebook

Contents

Foreword

We humans need and crave stability yet change continually lays waste to our best laid plans. This is an eternal and difficult truth for us. Achieving equanimity in the face of immutable change is the continual task of any spiritual quest. Hope is not only audacious, it is outrageous but crucial to achieve equanimity.

This struggle plays out in the attitudes and actions of a particular time and place by people who experienced a bitter war and an uneasy peace. Most North American and European readers may know of this conflict as the Southern Rhodesian Bush War which brought majority ruled Zimbabwe into existence. Yet the indigenous African majority call this war the *Chimurenga*. Many of the fictionalized stories in this book especially from the memories of the *Chimurenga* happened. The characters are representations of the amazing, generous, hospitable, and courageous people with whom I lived and worked for six years during the 1980s.

The following terms explain the historical and cultural background of these Shona villagers and their settler neighbours. More historical and cultural information are found in a glossary at the end of the novel. You will find English translations for Shona terms at the bottom of some pages.

chibharo – In pre-colonial times, this was communal work. However, during the Rhodesian regime, this was forced labour. Africans, who could not pay the numerous taxes for huts, chickens, pigs, etc., were forced to work on infrastructure projects by the Salisbury government. I knew older people in my village who were picked up by the army and carted off to labour camps where they would be taken to build highways, bridges and skyscrapers. The workers were fed and after three to six months, they received a few shillings to return home. During the serious drought years of 1962 and 63, many African peasant farmers were sent on chibharo.

Chimoio - a refugee camp in Mozambique in the area close to the eastern border of Zimbabwe. It was also used during the 1966-80 war as a training camp for ZANLA (Zimbabwean African National Liberation Army) fighters. ZANLA guerrillas mainly worked with the majority Shona population while the ZIPRA (Zimbabwean People's Liberation Army) generally worked among the minority Ndebele people.

chimurenga - war of liberation - Chimurenga I occurred between 1893-97. At the time a female spirit medium, who was possessed by the royal spirit Nehanda, prophesied that the Africans would learn to use the white man's weapons and defeat him in a second war. Her exact words were: "I will rise again."

This prophecy was fulfilled by Chimurenga II lasting from 1966-80. The Rhodesian government didn't concede that there was any civil unrest until 1974. Meanwhile the war raged in the rural areas where at that time 75 to 80% of the African population lived. The Smith regime was a clone of South African apartheid. Group Area acts etc. were in effect until 1980. Under Smith it would have been impossible and very illegal for Debbie Goerzen, a Canadian teacher, to even drink a beer with black colleagues in a public bar.

chimurenga name - all comrades had to adopt pseudonyms while they were in the bush and they never operated in their home areas to prevent government reprisals against their families and villages. Thus, Tawanda Murovi called himself the notorious one or *Chafichu*. Though he was from Chivi District, he operated in Chisungo.

comrade - is a term given to soldiers of the black nationalist groups. They borrowed the word comrade more from the Mozambique war for independence than the communist regimes in China than Russia. The comrades were also known as *vakomana*, or brothers and boys in the bush.

Initially ZANU PF (Zimbabwean African National Union) was a non-military civil rights organization who appealed to Britain and other Western countries to attempt a peaceful transfer to majority rule. Successive British governments chose to accept the settler regime's viewpoint. The British government trusted a garbled translation of the Shona Chief's Report to the Pierce Commission in 1972. For eye witness accounts see Lawrence Vambe, *An Ill-Fated People* (1973) and Judy Todd, *An Act of Treason: Rhodesia* (1965). For an excellent history of the propaganda war between the Rhodesian government and the African nationalist groups see Julie Frederikse, *None But Ourselves* (1984). For traditional Shona culture and the history of Great Zimbabwe see *Dzimbahwe: life and politics in the golden age 1100-1500 A.D.* (1983) by Kenneth Mufuka, Director of Museums during the 1980s.

The hardest bone of contention to the African nationalist movement and the land loving African majority was the hated Land Appointments Act of 1931. The white regime legalized the allocation of the most arable land for white settlers, thereby evicting the legitimate owners. This is how Van der Merwe's grandfather got Happy Valley from the Majira people of eastern Gutu. Because ZANU PF in exile received materiel and money from eastern bloc countries, especially China, Bulgaria and Rumania, socialist nomenclature was widely used in Zimbabwe during the years 1980 through to the middle 1990s. Also, comrade is a very close translation to the Shona word *shamwari* – friend.

Mwari - God. The Shona are an ethical monotheistic people. Other names for God are the Creator of the Whole World and The Almighty. The ancestors or *Madzimu,* are intermediaries between the living and God.

Harsh experience of oppression and war mostly succeeds in taking the atheist out of the foxhole dweller. The socialist tenor of politically correct speech at that time belies the fact that even war veterans, comrades, were and are deeply religious people. Hence, their world view was and is a syncretic mix of missionary Christianity and the Shona Traditional Religion. Thus, no one questioned the practice of opening any workplace meeting, ceremony, or event with a prayer to either Jesus or *Mwari*.

Vancouver, British Columbia, 2017

This work is dedicated to *Mai* and *Baba* Jo who opened the door and to the People of Bikita Communal Lands who let in this stranger and honoured me with their friendship.

List of Characters in order of appearance:

In Shona society, a person has four different names used in different social contexts. In some social contexts, family, close friends, and neighbors addressed a person by his/her clan name. Any ZANLA (Zimbabwean African Liberation Army) veteran of the civil war or Chimurenga always had a pseudonym. Even today, veterans are still called by their Chimurenga name as a mark of respect.

Proper Name	Nickname/ Name	Clan Name Chimurenga	Work Name
Kudakwashe Chitombo	Kuda	Majira	Mr. Chitombo
Tatenda Makumbe	Kindo	Shumba	Mr. Makumbe
Tawanda Murovi	Chafichu	Shumba	Mr. Murovi
John Mc Abe	Johnny or Jay	---------	Mr. Mc Abe
Debbie Goerzen	Debbie	---------	Miss Goerzen
Felicity Mandebvu Mandebvu	Feli	Moyo	Miss
Solomon Urozvi	Chef	Dziva Hungwe	Mr. Urozvi
Mathias Van der Merwe der Merwe	Matty or Mat	*Murimi we Mombe*	Mr. Van
Joshua Dube		Dziva Hungwe	Mr. Dube
Bill Fox	Wild Bill	----------	Mr. Fox

Chapter 1   Chisungo - We Are Together

A miracle! Two buses going through Chisungo Communal Lands competed for passengers.

Kudakwashe Chitombo smirked. For once he would get to work less than quickly but a little faster than a snail. *Maybe the prime minister was going to speak at Chisungo Office or something with the way people were pushing and shoving to board the two buses.* He thought.

But no, it was the day before schools opened. Khaki- uniformed teens were throwing their black steel trunks on top of the buses as acrobatic bus conductors scrambled up and down the moving vehicles tossing and kicking luggage. One smart-tongued boy shouted. "Hey *shamwaris*, playing Gweru United with mangos?"

"*Futsek, infana*", snarled a besieged conductor.

Kudakwashe shifted his travelling bag and watched anxiously as his new Chesterfield stereo perilously hovered to the top of a Shu-shine bus. Manyanye and Shu-Shine bus drivers revved their engines to attract Chisungo-bound passengers. Thick black smoke of worn down Shu-shine pistons cloaked the station.

Ragged little kids steered rusty wheelbarrows overflowing with bananas, oranges, apples, and cans of monkey nuts and groundnuts. The boys shouted after would-be customers. "Orange, banana, apple, *nyimo, nyino*. Ten cents, one shilling, *chete*!

Futsek infana – Get lost, kid!   *nyimo* – monkey oranges
chete - only

The town bus station, crowded on quieter days, now swarmed. Kuda stated his destination and boarded the Shu-shine bus. Navigating the crammed aisles amounted to an Olympic test of balance for most folks used the narrow row between thinly upholstered seats as a luggage compartment. He scrambled over jute bags of maize, buckets of fruit, bags of bread, suitcases, and canvas bags bulging with blankets, empty bottles and rolled reed mats.

Kudakwashe, known by his friends as Kuda, headed for the back, the drunkard section. He squished by watch battery salesmen, ice cream vendors and a blind female beggar with her baby on her back. The thirsty ones collided with Kuda to dash out to the bottle store to get just one quart of Castle lager to see them through to the next pit stop. He squeezed by the especially corpulent beggar who whined the usual, *"Kumbira batsirai,"* (please give me help), shaking two pennies in her chipped enamel dish; meanwhile, "cones, thirty cents, cones, watch battery, pen light, buy battery."

Finding an empty seat at the back, Kuda pulled a tepid quart of Castle out of his canvas bag and opened the bottle on the window sill. After fifteen minutes of revving and belching smoke, the bus wove its way through the masses and out of the terminus. He leaned back and closed his eyes letting the lukewarm beer slide down his throat.

An ex-footballer, Kudakwashe still carried his five foot ten girth well. He did most things like drinking, womanizing and making decisions with ponderous deliberation. His judgement seldom failed. And like most Shona, it took a major calamity, like his stereo meeting an untimely demise, tortuous frustration or a state of siege to raise his ire. He would not open his eyes until the disturbing rectangles of town slipped by and they were in open country.

Not that the sight of sand-choked streams, gaunt trees, and bony cows foraging the few bits of dry grass on the roadside were pleasing. His own *kraal* was nearly empty of cattle. The bare and rocky hills of Gutu District which his family called home were unmerciful at most times. But in the last three years, they were very cruel. If it weren't for the monthly government stipend of maize and beans, most people would be dead by now. But these short rations only kept them existing. "Thank God I'm qualified and working," he sighed. His family was better off.

Silently Kuda mused. *Three years of retribution, yes. If men spilled blood on the earth, God would punish them. That's what the spirit mediums and the old people said.* In this supposed rainy season, a baboon family leisurely loped across the cracked bed of the Mtilikwe River.

He shook his head. *Was God going to shut up the sky for a fourth year? Were too many clans destroyed during the war? I almost question why we ever fought the white man if drought was our only reward?*

A few minutes later, the bus screeched to a stop at Gutu turn off. Two dusty men thankfully boarded. Recognising his mates, Kuda shouted out the window.

"Hey, comrades, come over this side." His friends and workmates Tatenda Makumbe and Tawanda Murovi raced each other to the back. The slapped hands and triple handshakes of old friends woke up an old man sitting behind Kudakwashe.

Tatenda calling himself Kindo was as tall as

Chitombo but of lighter frame. Unlike Kuda however, Kindo was flighty and prone to frenzy. Most young men at this time sported beards and the three friends were no exception. While Kuda's mane was big and bushy, Kindo's was wispy. Styling himself after Kung Fu star, Bruce Lee, Kindo wore an expensive, brown, three-piece suit.

The third and most unusual of the trio, Tawanda Murovi, was a close cousin of Kindo. Both hailed from the same clan and area of Chivi District. Murovi was short, compact and muscular: one of those small toughs who would make a very unpleasant acquaintance in any dark alley. His brown complexion charred ebony from four years in the bush creased into many wrinkles with his routine jests. His deep brown eyes sat in slanted folds like many *Karangas*. Medium lips and a cute goatee displayed the trickster.

Murovi still kept his *Chimurenga* name – nom de guerre - Chafichu - the notorious one. His ex-combatant outfit: fading black beret, t-shirt, green army trousers and shiny, maroon boots bequeathed from a dead Rhodesian African Rifles soldier belied a sharp intelligence. His dark eyes bored into opponents and students alike. Chafichu was the wild intellectual of the troupe as Kindo was the buffoon and Kuda the leader.

"Hey *blas* how's it?" Chafichu happily squeezed next to Kudakwashe. Across the aisle Kindo's legs straddled wide.

Kindo leaned over and gushed, "Guess what? *Murimi we Mombe* the Boer Van der Merwe gave us a lift!" Chafichu sniggered.

blas – Shona-English – pal   *ambuya* – grandmother

"Come on, no ways, "Kuda sneered. For three generations Chitombo's family worked for Murimi we

Mombe, Mathias Van der Merwe's family. As a young bride Kuda's grandmother watched the first white men come over the hills from South Africa in 1920. One of them was Mathias Van der Merwe's father.

Kuda's earliest memory was straddling his mother's back as she trod to the fields to toil for Murimi's father. A hulk of a man with a big stomach, the giant rode a towering metal ox with big round wheels. The old man Paul Van der Merwe was liberal with his horsewhip on animals and humans alike. Kuda's people existed in terror of it. At night in their hovel his father, Rungamai, and the other men would tell shivery stories of the exploits and cruelties of the big baas, *Va Tumbu*, Mr. Stomach.

A later memory: Kuda and his younger brother, Tererai, snuck through the khaki grass peering between the blades to watch a couple of labourers tilling illegal food crops. Kuda's grandmother, *Ambuya* Chitombo, who worked at the house, regaled the family with the latest scene of Mr. Stomach eating his way through two chickens. He was more hyena than man but a very fat one.

Then one afternoon Va Tumbu stood in the barnyard screaming at Kuda's father who stood defiantly looking into the eyes of the Boer. He lashed his whip in the air as he threatened to beat *Ambuya*, Kuda's grandmother. "You get out of my way, kaffir."

"You are not going to touch my mother." Mr. Chitombo stared down his assailant. *In his mind, he desperately sought courage from his ancestors. He would not hit the baas; that meant death to him and*

14

there was no one to keep his family. But he would not run away. Nor would he allow this madman to assault his mother.

Paul Van der Merwe yelled, "That bitch stole money from my house!"

Rungamai Chitombo's fear turned to anger, then rebellion. "My mother is not an animal and you will not touch her."

"You insolent black bastard! How dare you tell me what to do!" The Boer raged.

"If you do not know by now who is the thief and who isn't, then you are a fool." With that Kuda's father walked away from the maniacal farmer who was raising his whip. It struck *Baba* Kuda's back, tearing his overalls, but he kept on walking. Then Mathias Van der Merwe, who was fresh from college, rushed over to see his old playmate bleeding. The old man had gone too far once too often. The younger Van der Merwe leapt at his father and they struggled for the weapon.

"Pa, are you crazy? Leave him alone, for Chrissakes" Go home and rest. Let me handle this." Mr. Stomach scowled at his son who threw the whip into a haystack.

That night, as she applied herbs on her husband's back, *Mai* Kuda said, "Why doesn't that idiot sit in the shade like other old men and stop running around confusing people."

The next day Mr. Van der Merwe senior sacked Mr. Chitombo from his job. No other farmer would hire the mechanic because he was labelled a troublemaker.

Next came the years of harsh poverty in the tribal trust lands. The tribes were kept in trust that they would reach a level of half-starved weakness. Then they would succumb to whatever the regime demanded, including *chibharo*. What was traditionally community service, during Rhodesian rule it became forced labour building the white man's highways and high buildings.

When Kuda was in standard four, Va Tumbu died. Four days later the young baas, Mathias, came to their compound. The only no-knees, white men, who ever got into the bush were the missionaries. What was this Boer doing here? As tradition dictated, Mr. Chitombo invited Mr. Van der Merwe into the *hozi*. Kuda crept up to the doorway to listen.

Both men spoke *ChiKaranga*, the Shona of the south-central clans. After the traditional greetings and passing news of their families, Mathias Van der Merwe offered,

"Well, Father of Kudakwashe, I want you to come back and work for me. I had three idiots who didn't know a spark plug from their assholes."

Chitombo laughed. But he was careful. This was no longer his boyhood friend who used to call him *shanwari yapamoyo*, but baas.

"I was chased. Why do you want me back?"

"It was my father who chased you, not me. Also, I

Baba Kuda – father of Kuda   *Mai Kuda* – mother of Kuda

hozi – welcome hut, the front parlour of a Shona compound

shamwari yapa moyo – friend of the heart- bosom buddy

found out that the cook boy, who drank seven day's beer, he stole the money."

Baba Kuda knew that one day the old baas would eat and drink himself into the grave and that judging from his character and actions the young baas, would come to see him. He wondered what it would be like to work for Mathias. Chitombo was clear about a few things; however, so he devised a plan.

"All right, Mr. Van der Merwe, I will come back to work for you on these four conditions: 1) I want to build a decent house for my family, 2) I want three pounds a month, African mechanic's wages, 3) I want to have my own vegetable garden, 4) My sons will go to school. They can work for you during holidays." Chitombo waited.

So did Van der Merwe. He recognised that the African talked sense. At Gwebe College, he learned that consideration of skill made more financial sense than consideration of race and the Boer needed Rungamai's skill to overhaul and maintain his machinery. Van der Merwe costed out his options *He knew he would pay dearly for a European mechanic of unknown ability. He had two domestics: Ambuya Chitombo and a teenaged girl working in the house at one pound a month each and five other men in the fields. Total labour cost 17 pounds a month. What were three more pounds when his farm was bringing in more than one hundred and fifty a month?*

The Boer measured his response, for in Rhodesia decency was an act of courage fraught with subtle and more obvious consequences even for Europeans. "You're a hard man to please. But it's fair enough. You have a week to build your compound. Then you can begin to overhaul the Massey's engine."

Rungamai Chitombo looked down at his hands. He said softly, "That's all right. I will come."

Very few Africans at that time would have stood up to the Boers like Baba Kuda did. He was a man of integrity and Kudakwashe revered him. The present tense shook Kuda's shoulder.

Chafichu grinned at him. "Ya, I even sat BESIDE him."

In mock solemnity Kuda reverted to the vernacular, the haunting and melodic zvv, zhh, and svvs of deep Karanga Shona.

"Ah, Notorious One, you are too cruel. How did Farmer of Cattles react?"

"This is Zimbabwe. How is anyone supposed to react? He chose to pick us. He could have passed us, you know." Chafichu then extracted a crumpled package of Kingsgate filters from the sleeve of his t-shirt, checked his thigh pocket for a match and found fluff balls. "Hey, Kuda, give me some fire."

Chitombo handed him a box of matches. Chafichu puffed long and hard and kept them.

"Ah, ah, you, give my motherless matches back." Kuda stuck out his big paw. "Invest three cents, you cheap kid."

"Sorry, *blas*. Old habits die hard. How is your family, anyway?"

"They're okay. But my grandmother's sick nowadays."

"Sorry to hear that." Both Chafichu and Kindo frowned.

"What's wrong with her?" Kindo asked.

"Ah, her body is falling apart. She is getting very old."

The trio kept quiet for a long time. Kindo broiled in his heavy suit. He took off the jacket and the sleeve caught on Chafichu's cigarette. Sparks flew inside the coat.

"Baboon, you are burning my three-hundred-dollar suit." Kindo was annoyed.

"Little brother, dress for the weather not an advertisement." Chafichu inspected the sleeve. "No damage."

"You are too lucky," Kindo threatened.

"Sometimes I think you are mad, Makumbe. Why do you spend so much beer money on blankets for?"

"I'm a star. That's why, you tattered beggar."

Chafichu was too used to Kindo's protests. He laughed and pretended to slit his friend's throat.

"Hey chaps," Kuda said in English. "We are passing Rhodesia."

Chafichu's face hardened when he saw the Club's white two storeys surrounded by tennis courts and bowls greens.

"You know the only time I ever get in there is with either Debbie or old man Urozvi," he said quietly.

"You think she will come back from the Christmas holidays?" Kindo asked.

Kuda explained, "Why not? She is not finished her contract yet. And if she absconds back to Canada, I will personally send poison in the mail to her. She'll wreck my department if she keeps away."

"For a white, she is somehow good." Kindo supported her.

"I don't know about that," Chafichu said thoughtfully. "She hasn't proved herself yet."

"I think she says what she really means better than John Macabe who says very little. And I don't know whose side he is on," Kindo re-joined, again in a pensive tone. He liked Johnny to some extent. They shared a rabid love of football and an intense intellectual curiosity. Kindo loved numbers and Johnny was an amateur bone collector. Johnny dithered while Debbie made clear choices.

"Tatenda, what is wrong with Johnny," Kuda asked.

"He's too, you know, I cannot quite put my finger on it. He's usually sensible. But somehow I think he is confused because he says one thing to we Africans and another to the Europeans."

"Kuda brooded into his beard. "I think he is very innocent. And I am afraid that he can be led astray, if you know what I mean."

"Tch, He already has," Kindo offered sadly. *Baba* Tavonga, the bartender, told me that he is starting to go to the Club every day and not with us. He saw Johnny

20

drinking with a white man who is a supervisor at the mine."

"Our comrade Macabe is no longer a comrade. He is falling into their net," Kudakwashe surmised. He was visibly relieved to see that they had passed by *Mai* Rushai's bottle store, a big blue building set back from the main road.

The stubby grass and expansive fields of the large farms gave way to the thatched round houses and terraced fields of the communal farmers. Dozens of Scotch carts, drawn by scrawny oxen, wheelbarrows and skinny donkeys with empty jute sacks followed by expectant people crowded the edge of the road. A stunned cow escaped onto the tarmac. The bus swerved around it and Chitombo screamed out the window.

"*Infana, buda mugwagawa!*" The confused herd boy looked up at the speeding bus. "Hey kid, you want a translation? Get off the road!"

"Chitombo, you are an elitist," Chafichu chuckled.

"*Futsek*, man. I just got a new stereo on the top of this thing and I don't want a cow to make my life ironical."

"Ah, what is boiling your porridge, just now? Leave fools to their folly."

"Not when it affects me, Mr. Chafichu Murovi."

"Who cares," mouthed Kindo. "You chaps want to get into the shop and play some slug?"

"Na," said Kuda. "I want to get some boys to help me home with the stereo. Maybe you guys can pass through my place to hear it."

"No sweat," Chafichu eagerly accepted the invitation.

Msassa Mountain now beckoned them with its friendly bulk. Toting their bags, the threesome pushed their way to the front.

"*Chose* Station. *Chose!*" The conductor cried above the hubbub.

Chapter 2   The *Povos*

Wheva, the morning star, pulled the sun out of bed and the fiery disk ploughed the furrows of night churning up rows of bleeding light which streamed into the bedroom window. Kindo squinted at the haemorrhaging clouds and hoped that they might bring rain this day. He rolled over and snuggled against his wife.

"Ma."

"Ugh," she grumbled and burrowed herself deeper into the sheets.

"Mother of Panashe, tea."

"Dad, I'm tired."

"Ah, ah. As your lord and master, I command you to boil the kettle." His authoritative tone soon gave way to a plaintive whine as a drum pounded louder against the inside of his skull.

"Mr. Makumbe, boil it yourself."

"But I am weak from hangover." He moaned.

"So what, I have been up with Panashe half the night. He was colicky."

"He is sleeping now." Kindo muttered. She ignored him and yawned.

"So, I don't get breakfast?" The lord and master pouted on the side of the bed.

"You won't die from lighting the stove."

"But I will. My head is splitting like burning firewood." He dramatically groaned as he clutched his head as if the pain were excruciating, which it nearly was.

She chuckled at his pitiful pantomime with not a shred of sympathy. "Fool, you were drunk with Murovi and Chitombo last night. This is your punishment." She buried further into the cocoon of their mahogany double bed. Kindo forked out one hundred dollars a month for this luxury on a hire purchase account at OK Bazaar in town.

Then ten-month-old Panashe began to whimper from his crib in the corner. She got up and nestled the baby in her arms. "Dad, Panashe wants breakfast too. Can you get me a glass of milk, please?"

Kindo groggily shook his head but that became too agonizing. He winced and remembered some conveniently forgotten reverend calling St. Castle the devil's brew. He sighed and gazed at his wife.

Qualified primary teacher - No way my mother would talk to my father like that without a beating. He muttered to himself. But Kindo was a marshmallow. "The liberated African woman," he grumbled a little louder as he pulled on a pair of trousers and shuffled toward the kitchen.

Like most married cottages at the mission, the Makumbe residence boasted two bedrooms, a rather spacious sitting room, kitchen and separated toilet and shower. Ceilings graced both bedrooms and the front room. But in the rest of the house naked tin sizzled in summer and chilled in winter and on cool mornings like this one. He fished for a long butt in the ashtray in the sitting room. He lit it on the glowing embers in the cast-iron stove in the kitchen. Kindo threw on more kindling

24

and a sizable chunk of *msassa* wood, a gnarled but sturdy little tree which turned red in the springtime. It heavily populated the mountain above the school and provided the nearest source of firewood.

Cool water spraying into a yellow enamel kettle woke him up completely. Inhaling deeply on the butt, he tried not to think of the icy shower that would splatter him into a colder sobriety.

The loud suckling and smacking from the bedroom signalled that his son was just as hungry as he was. When Panashe fed at his mother's breast, a thickness arose in Kindo's throat. It was the most beautiful sound he had ever known. Baba Panashe was sorry that he had been so harsh with her so early. *I will bring her some tea and bread,* he promised himself. *Oh, yes, she wanted some milk.* He mixed some powdered Nestlé's with boiled water from the fridge. *A nice plate would serve as a tray for the glass.*

"Your milk, Madam."

She sipped greedily. "Thank you, Sir. I see that you are now human and not bush dog."

He laughed at her white moustache. "I just woke up. Putting on the kettle only sustained minor injuries to my Kung Fu arm." He smiled.

"What do you want for breakfast, Tatenda?"

"Do we have any eggs left?"

"Eh, heh, the layers are working overtime nowadays."

"Good, I will go and take my bath." He kissed her and felt the warm cheek of his son. She ran her fingers through his soft beard.

"Don't fall into the drain," she laughed.

Under the shower Kindo soaped himself down and for the fiftieth time realized how much he loved his small family. If something or someone came to disturb or hurt them, it would be like a hyena tearing out his heart.

Two houses along the road in what was called Teachers' Row or the Ghetto, Kudakwashe yawned and sadly looked at the empty space beside him. His wife was studying at the commercial college in Gweru. Then the thought of her visit next weekend lifted his mood and he happily sang out to his youngest sister, Chiedza, who was already busying herself in the kitchen.

"Good morning, Sissy. Are the boys up yet?

"Good morning, Elder Brother, they're still fast asleep. Did you sleep well?" She entered the doorway and smiled at Kuda, who was paying her school fees.

"I slept. How did you like my new stereo," he asked expectantly.

"Ah, it is fine, Kuda. Can I put on Radio Three?"

"Sure, after you get me a coffee." He stretched, got out of bed adjusting his crumpled pyjamas.

Just next door, in his cluttered but tidy living room, Tawanda a.k.a. Chafichu was fully dressed in a khaki shirt and green drill pants with the omnipresent beret. A red pen stuck out of his shirt pocket. He gulped the dregs of his tea trying to lick the sugar residue. He had a three-teaspoon habit. Two open plan books mocked his frown: one for History, the other for Shona.

Twelve empty beer bottles, half a kilogram of maize meal, two oozing tomatoes, and some sprouting onions graced his bachelor's pantry. The fridge boasted mangled margarine, half a loaf of stale bread, dried meat in a blue enamel dish, sugar and tea. Tawanda didn't like ants in his sugar.

In the living room two piles of novels and an impressive stack of hard-cover volumes sprawled on the floor beside his stereo. This million-watt system gave epileptic fits to the ancestors every Saturday night. Yet it was all too solitary. His twenties were fleeing like kudu from a brush fire and it was high time he looked for a decent wife to cook him a nutritious breakfast. His usual liaisons were the raw harlots who couldn't make it in the towns so they prowled the rural bottle stores for customers. He never got breakfast.

Ya, a nice girl from a good family who knows how to take care of a man properly: then I can start to have sons, he thought.

Hangovers usually made Chafichu philosophical. Of all the places he had slept in, and some of them were very strange, this concrete block house on Teacher's Row was the best. He remembered sharing a mud-walled bedroom with his brothers at home in Chivi, the noisy bedbug ridden dormitories of his secondary school days, the posh double rooms of his two years at Gokomere Mission doing his A-levels, and the cold, damp, puffy-face-in-the morning years in the bush. From the Inyanga border in the Eastern Highlands, to Chimoio ZANLA army camp, to an army camp in Tanzania, forest copses, caves, trees, and oh, he revelled in the luxury of someone's mud hut with a red mat! From the dry scrub land in Shangaani country just north of Hippo Valley Estates, through Matsai, north through the cattle country in Nyajena, the forests of Chief Ziki's area and east to the farmlands of Chief Dhuma's domain, Chafichu knew Chisungo Communal Lands like his own heartbeat. He had come to love these simple folks who risked everything for him and the other comrades. Here the hills were greener, the women prettier and even the witches were more peaceful: they only sent spirits or dashed poison in one's beer - a very amenable place to be. In Zaka the wizards sent lightning to their enemies and in his *musha*, home village in Chivi, vengeful spirits possessed cows.

Checking his digital watch, he turned on the six-thirty news. The tinny Voice of Zimbabwe did not entertain him this morning: the usual diatribe against the apartheid racist regime in South Africa. Chafichu wondered *why didn't the leaders of the OAU just send all their armies down there to slaughter the Boers, instead of talk talk talk.* He slouched out the door, locked it and put the key on the top door jamb so the house girl could find it later that morning.

Chapter Three   Meetings

As Chafichu walked towards the school, Kuda and Kindo were already on the road. They all shook hands and strolled leisurely toward the school. John Macabe joined them.

Sunning themselves by the headmaster's office, Debbie Goerzen, the Canadian English teacher and Felicity Mandebvu, the Domestic Science teacher, saw the foursome sauntering across the bare compound.

"Here come the Ghetto Boys from lowest *Chitungwiza*," Debbie shouted at them. Mandebvu giggled. Bright smiles lit the men's faces. Predictably Chafichu called back.

"Debbie, when did you return from the townships in Harare? And how is life with the baboons on Mount Pleasant?"

"Last night Mr. and Mrs. B. Baboon rudely came to dine in my spinach patch."

"And did they enjoy their meal?"

"The cats didn't let them," she grinned proudly.

"Kill them slowly," John Macabe, the quintessential cat hater muttered.

"Who," Debbie knew what he meant but she wanted him to display his callousness towards her beloved watch cats.

"Those flea bags you call your pets," he answered grumpily.

Equally unimpressed with cats sitting on Debbie's

dining room table, Chafichu snickered. "Forget, she wouldn't get two cents for their meat from the Cold Storage Commission."

At this point Kindo moaned, "The chef is too cruel. Imagine a seven-a.m. meeting."

"Too early for you Mr. Makumbe?" The headmaster loomed over the senior Math master. The intimidation was increased by the fact that the portly administrator stood about two feet above Kindo on the cement steps of his office.

Kindo wheedled, "Just a joke, Sir. I always like getting up before the chickens with a headache."

"Who has the headache, you or the chickens? Take two aspirin and see me in my office next time you have *babalazi*, Kindo."

While Makumbe slunk into the staffroom, the headmaster motioned Chafichu into his office. Taking his seat behind a large, cluttered desk, Headmaster Solomon Urozvi motioned Chafichu Murovi into a chair.

"Good Morning, Mr. Murovi."

Chafichu was confused. *Why did the old man want to talk to him while the other teachers waited in the staff room?* His bush senses rose to alert levels as the familiar cold feeling crept into his veins like ants walking over his legs on a damp, winter morning when the *Guti* winds blew in the fog. Chafichu knew he was in shit but he couldn't figure out why?

"Good morning, Sir. How was your holiday?"

babalazi - hangover

30

"Very nice, and yours?" Urozvi read the fear in the young man's eyes. *Good, he may be receptive to correction.*

"Very good, Sir. I visited my eldest brother in Mutare and then my parents in Chivi."

"So, you are well rested and ready for the new school year. Before that can start, we need to discuss something that happened last term."

"Chef?" Chafichu inquired.

"I think you know what I am talking about."

"No, Sir."

"All right, young man, I will come to the point. I received a letter of complaint about you from one of our parents, Mr. Machingadzi. Have you heard of him?

"Yes, he is the father of Yasser Arafat, one of my form three boys. He passes into form four this term."

"Do you have any idea why Mr. Machingadzi would complain about you/"

Chafichu was dumbfounded. The only altercation he had with this notoriously wild student was the breast in the Bible incident. But the headmaster knew about this. How had a simple disciplinary matter come back to haunt him?

"Did this have anything to do with the justified beating I gave him and Gabriel Manyanye? I caught them during afternoon study drawing female breasts in their bibles. The pictures were in Luke Chapter 5.

"The deputy headmaster was there as a witness as

per regulations." Chafichu defended his actions.

"Unfortunately, you were following outdated regulations." The headmaster countered. "Didn't you remember that the Permanent Secretary of Education for Masvingo Province stated in the March 1983 Circular that corporal punishment was deemed to be educationally unsound and should not occur in the schools?

"And did we not discuss this new regulation in a special called Staff Meeting of Friday April 1?"

"I thought it was an April fool's joke." Chafichu nervously tittered.

Urozvi quietly fumed, "Young man, sometimes you are too funny for nothing. I find that comment very rude. Haven't you read any psychology? We are educators, not torturers."

Chafichu wanted to hide in a convenient cave. "I'm so sorry, Sir. I didn't mean to make a joke. I was nervous. But did you also receive a letter from the Manyanye family?"

"No," the headmaster muttered, "When I broached the topic with Mr. Manyanye in this office, he complained that you didn't beat his son hard enough." Urozvi was annoyed by the simple but devastating question. *Murovi should have studied law.*

"But that doesn't matter what Mr. Manyanye thinks, your actions were against current regulations for last year and Mr. Machingadzi quoted them in his letter. You know he works for the Permanent Secretary in Masvingo."

"I heard something like that," Chafichu answered and not only did he see the flaw in Urozvi's argument, the mistake angered him. "However, I find it interesting that you are dismissing what Mr. Manyanye, a local farmer, says and clinging to what semi-chef like Mr. Machingadzi says.

"In fact, you and I are seated here in this office because of the sacrifices made during the war by Mr. Manyanye and other *povos* like him. Also, the povos are closer to our African traditions than the bureaucrats in town who used to work for Ian Smith's government.

"Why should I pay attention to a *mutengesi* who knows nothing of the suffering of our people? Does this mean that our situation has not changed, except that African chefs have replaced white Rhodesians? I do not agree with beating people for no reason. Yet I will give out quick justice when it is needed."

Urozvi listened as he tapped his fingers on the desk. Impervious to the headmaster's irritation, Murovi soldiered on.

"Mr. Machingadzi wants to ignore the fact that his son is a juvenile delinquent. Didn't Miss Goerzen and I discover the shebeen he was running in the boys' dormitory and was he not also importing *mahures* from Mai Rushai's bottle store? This boy is a crook and he has no respect for our traditions or the laws of this mission school if he can sell liquor and women. And did not his father call you and me liars when you wanted to suspend

mutengesi – sell out, collaborator with the settler regime.

povos – local people who supported the comrades

mahures – prostitutes

Yasser Arafat last year for those actions against school regulations?

Urozvi knew enough about the facts mentioned in this latest of Chafichu Murovi's routine rants. The headmaster waited.

"Now, Mr. Urozvi, I respect you as my headmaster. I will follow what you tell me to do because I know that you defend the best interests of the students who want to learn. But I cannot follow the dictates of the semi-chef who won't correct his own son.

"I ask you, Sir. What will you do next time Yasser Arafat Machingadzi does another funny performance?"

Though British educated with pretensions to gentility and still a member of that race of pot-bellied and timid men who survived the Bantu Education System, the headmaster of Chose Secondary could see the hypocrisy of wild boy's parent. *Urozvi also knew and subscribed to the tradition that Shona elders were responsible for the actions of their family members. Mr. Machingadzi was probably a typical town man who was not taking responsibility for his son.*

"Mr. Murovi, you argue well, but I caution you to take care when dealing with someone like Mr. Machingadzi who has much boot in this province.

"Fortunately for both of us, this week the Comrade Minister Himself had a temper tantrum and said to the Bulawayo Chronicle that teachers should beat stubborn students. So, you are off the hook, so to speak. I was going to ask you to write a letter of apology but since the Minister has spoken, I will remind Mr. Machingadzi about the new regulation and also remind him that his son is on last warning to be suspended from this school."

Relieved, Chafichu clapped hands in respectful thanks and joined his colleagues in the staff room. For his part, Urozvi sat for a few minutes digesting the twists and turns of the dramatic meeting with the irrepressible Cde. Chafichu Murovi. It seemed to the headmaster that he was one who was corrected.

The staffroom décor included two large wooden tables boasting decades of scratched in messages and signatures. A number of chalk boxes were seconded as ashtrays. The headmaster took his place at the end of one table while the Miss Mandebvu, read a verse from Proverbs while the rest of the staff gradually woke up.

"Welcome back, Gentlemen and Ladies. I trust that all of you are in good health to tackle this New Year. It seems that one of our senior masters was bitterly complaining about the ungodly hour of this meeting."

Kindo wanted to dissolve into a nearby pit. Seventeen pairs of eyes grinned at him.

"Unfortunately," Mr. Urozvi went on, "we have a lot of ground to cover. Would the secretary read the minutes of the December 1983 meeting?" Mrs. Mandebvu quickly read off the points.

"All in favour that the minutes are correct and in full."

Silence. Most folded and their arms and dozed. The chef cleared his throat.

"Well, that's unanimous approval. Would someone like to move the minutes read?"

The Agriculture master, Manasseh Chidhuma, raised his finger.

"Thank you, Mr. Chidhuma. Seconders?" Kuda wearily raised his arm.

"Thank you, Mr. Chitombo. Now for the agenda: 1) Timetable slash subject allocation, 2) Discipline, 3) Sports, 4) Announcements slash CIRCULARS, 5) New business. That's all I came up with. Does any member want to add something?"

"Yeah," Johnny muttered into his palm.

"Mr. Macabe?"

"How about Tea Club?"

"All right, that goes under new business. Anything else?"

Silence. Everyone was just a little ticked off with Johnny for prolonging the torture. A bird twittered in one of the gum trees behind the building.

"Very good, again unanimous support." Kindo began to snore. The chef glanced over his thick glasses. "Mr. Makumbe do I detect that as an additional statement?"

Kuda then kicked his mate under the table. "*Iwe*, I bruise easily," Kindo growled."

"Hm hm, Mr. Makumbe?"

"I second the motion, Sir."

iwe – informal you used between friends and subordinates

"Thank you," the headmaster drawled. "Now for item 1) as for subject allocation, I am glad that all of you

36

have returned this year so the subjects will be the same. Except that each of you will follow your classes. For example: Mr. Murovi will now teach form four Shona and form two History. Miss Goerzen will take form four English and form four Education for Living."

Someone mumbled, "Education for Reproduction." A titter ran through the staff and the headmaster patiently continued.

"Any other teachers who need advice on their subjects should consult their head of department." The spine of Chose Secondary, each vertebra, once again slumped over in repose.

"Item 1a. – Timetable. So, Mr. Murovi and Mr. Chitombo?"

"Ah, no, Chef." Chafichu shook his head vigorously.

"I beg your pardon, Mr. Murovi?"

"I cannot do it."

"Explain, please. You have been doing a good job."

"After Kuda and I put together the exam timetable last term, some of our dear comrades here, were, ah, displeased. In fact, I received two threatening letters at my house from anonymous sources of course.

"The timetable was defaced beyond recognition with red ink. And at the end a certain comrade, whose name I will not mention, aimed a knife at me at Mai Rushai's bottle store. Ccl, that is very poor. I am no longer interested in this martyrdom committee."

"These are very serious charges, young man. Why didn't you report this?"

"Ah, NO!" Cephas Tafunga tore open his sports shirt, spoiling for battle. Chafichu rolled up his sleeves and took off his watch.

Tafunga shouted, "Name names, you coward!" Suddenly, all the recumbent vertebrae got a shot of adrenaline. So, the staff meeting was going to get interesting after all.

"Withdraw that statement, Tafunga," Chafichu clenched his fists ready to spring. "If you think you can do a better job, then do it! I am not coming under your knife again. And you better withdraw your first statement."

Tafunga folded his arms defiantly. The chef took off his bulky tweed jacket as the sun was beginning to warm up the dim room.

"Stop this, both of you!" The old man's blood pressure began to rise with the promise of action. "Don't you have any professional decorum?"

Suddenly a well-timed fart polluted the tense atmosphere. A cloud of rotten eggs enveloped the company. Everyone held noses and laughed the adversaries down. Somebody opened a window. Catching his breath, Urozvi wiped away tears. He resumed his composure.

"Right, Mr. Tafunga, you are now the head of the Timetable Committee. And you will not revenge against Mr. Murovi or vice versa. Any complaints should be directed through the right channels."

"Humph, item 2 – discipline."

"Excuse me,"

"Yes, Miss Goerzen."

"All drunkards should be chased from boarding. Some of these guys are even running shebeens in the boys' dorm."

Kindo frantically waved his hand. "All form ones should be severely beaten for the first two months. That's to acclimatize them to our system/"

"Isn't that a little extreme, Mr. Makumbe?"

"No, Sir."

"Explain."

"Form ones are very stupid. In fact, any drunkard or crook with half a brain knows to keep away from Mai Naysha's on Friday nights. For example, last November Bornwell Tumbu and his thugs pitch up at the bottle store to do funny business. Unfortunately for them, about ten of us were there. Manasseh locked the door and we made them go through the line-up. We clapped them hard."

"Except me," Johnny exclaimed. "One poor kid about four feet tall went through everybody and when he got to me, he said, "Please, Sir, hit me on the other side of my face."

Kindo resumed," I propose, Sir, that Bornwell Tumbu be chased from the school. He is horrible. Ah, this kid is somehow a genius. He stole a hose from the junior

chibuku – local rapoko/maize beer   *ngozi* – evil spirit

39

lab and went to the side window of Mai Naysha's and siphoned gallons of *chibuku* into his mouth. He even disguised himself as an *ngozi* by putting on black clothes, black mask and carrying bows and arrows." Again, general laughter shared by the narrator.

"The Discipline Committee is well aware of Tumbu's case and he is on last warning," the chef answered.

"Shouldn't all kids caught drinking get one warning and get kicked out of boarding on the second offence?" Debbie ventured.

"That's all right. All in favour?" For once the spine straightened and each person raised a hand.

"Thank you, staff. Item 3 – Sports. Mr. Chitombo, I believe we have athletics this term. How are you going to organize your teams?"

"We will recruit from the form ones at our practice after general work every day. Sir, I have a request. Ah, we shouldn't allow those mad people from down down Chiredzi. Remember last year when the headmaster showed up with twenty other drunkards? They disturbed the game and at half time their whole team took a walk all over our goalie's face. I don't want my team to be used as pin cushions. And those rude people didn't even thank us for lunch!"

Kindo piped up. "Chef, these people are dangerous. We went there for a match and all the villagers showed up with spears and axes. They stoned our school truck and said we were not going to leave their place alive. I want them chucked from the Chisungo Sports Council."

"Ya, and if they ever get to this place again, I'm going to get some very rough comrades from the village Youth Brigade and we'll guard the field with AK 47s. Any of these raw people do funny business – bang! Finish!" Chafichu was enjoying his fantasy.

By this time, the short and peppery Manasseh, who vainly tried to grow a beard, stood and delivered his message like the brewer's son announcing that a new batch was ready for consumption. "Headlines Harare Herald: LINESMAN RUNS AMOK IN CHISUNGO!"

The chef impatiently tapped his gold Cross pen on the table top. "Gentlemen, please sit down. Mr. Murovi, we will not have weapons or Youth Brigades in attendance when we play other schools. And Mr. Chidhuma, we will not invite the Herald to record unofficial performances of humour. I will discuss this matter with the headmaster of *VaPenga* Secondary School."

For the next eon, the chef's Cambridge English droned through five pages of ministry CIRCULARS. By no means was Mr. Urozvi hated by anybody on staff; his imperious behavior was tolerated with good humor. Both parties tacitly agreed to tolerate the other's peccadilloes. He ranted and raved during meetings and teachers slept off their binges. But they awoke to do their jobs: thanks to the apartheid South African embargo, without enough textbooks, sewing machines, lab equipment, art supplies, sports equipment and teachers.

Five O-levels promoted a simple school child to the messiahship of his or her often poor family. Even if the reward was a low paid clerical post or temporary teaching job, the extra bags of maize at month-end, those packages of clothes and school fees for the younger siblings often launched a peasant family from desperation to hopeful struggle.

"Item 4A – Announcements: only one: Mr. Mathias Van der Merwe, otherwise known as *Murimi we Mombe,* will be guest preaching at church next Sunday. We all know of this local farmer and everyone who is interested are invited. Now Gentlemen and Ladies, I urge you to attend. It would be a nice gesture of reconciliation if we as a multiracial staff showed up."

Debbie evaded his glance by looking out the window. She had decamped from the conservative Mennonite church of her childhood when amongst other indignities, an elder laughed at the idea of a female pastor. Here she was again in the lap of a very patriarchal society. Urozvi was ok as far as headmasters went, but she would not attend a church that practiced apartheid of race or gender.

Johnny busily read a Harold Robbins novel. He reserved Sunday mornings for tennis and a full English breakfast at the Club.

Chafichu concentrated on burning holes into a chalk box. This triggered an old conundrum for him: *how could the Jesuits at Gokomere and the apartheid Dutch Reformed Church both claim Christianity as their faith?* "Murimi we Mombe preach anything sensible? I don't want to waste my time," he murmured.

"Item 5 – New Business Slash Tea Break. What did you want to say Mr. Macabe?"

"Now I don't want to insult anybody or cause bad feelings." Johnny exclaimed.

"But you are going to insult us anyway and cause bad feelings. Is that right, Comrade?" By now Chafichu

Murimi we Mombe – farmer of cows/ cattle

had his leg cocked up on a chair. Macabe did not like the way Murovi's eyes drilled into his motives. Johnny was six-foot-one with red hair and a beard covered half his freckled puffy face. Pale blue eyes, usually indirect, now showed irritation.

"I'm just tired of subsidizing people who won't pay for tea, yet they want to drink and eat for free."

"What do you propose, Mr. Macabe?" The chef was bracing himself for another fight.

"I suggest that only people who have paid their dues be allowed in the staff room for tea."

"I should think it would be better if we approach the delinquents to pay their subscriptions," the headmaster advised.

"What if they don't? I'm still going to be forced to support them."

"I don't think this is the proper place to discuss this. The organizers of the tea club should take up this one." Urozvi tried to diffuse the toxic brew.

"Meanwhile, I'm still going to have to fork out for people who are too cheap to part with five bucks of their booze money." Macabe refused to give up the bone of contention.

"Johnny, shut up." Debbie scolded him before any of the Zimbabweans did. He was going too far. Chafichu, Kudakwashe, Kindo and Manasseh glared at Johnny, but he didn't raise his eyes to look at the faces of his colleagues. Johnny misunderstood their silence for acquiescence, admission of defeat.

"We will discuss this at a more opportune time, Mr. Macabe." The headmaster wanted to avoid this volatile situation through quiet diplomacy with the non-payers.

"The meeting is now adjourned," he finally announced. Everyone breathed a sigh of release. Another performance was over until next month.

Debbie caught up to Johnny as he was quickly striding away.

"John, I think we better have a talk."

He barked at her, "Don't bother! You're always on their side anyway."

"There is no us and them. We're just human beings trying to work with each other. Sometimes people make mistakes."

"I don't want to hear about it. Just leave me alone for now. Okay?" He stalked off.

Chafichu came up behind Debbie. "Sissy, don't worry about him. He is bad tempered."

"He shouldn't talk like that. And we all know that he's trying to attack you and Kuda. What's between you guys, anyway?"

"Ah, just some beer talk. But he's right in a way that some of us haven't paid for our tea in December or November."

"*Iwe*, you're making a good salary." Now Debbie was getting annoyed.

"True. But I have a lot of accounts and I am also

sending two youngsters through secondary school. *Saka,* that means that I have to decide between going to the pub and having tea at school.

"You didn't have to buy all that furniture last year, you know."

"But I had to." He explained. "How else am I going to attract a decent wife? Soon as I pay off the furniture, I have to start saving *rora.* You think a woman with any brain is going to marry a beggar with a transistor radio and a paraffin stove?"

"I wouldn't care about that sort of thing."

He laughed, "Good, let's get married."

She stuck out her hand, "That'll cost you fifty cows, buddy."

"Ah, you are too expensive. I hope some woman's family will charge me only ten cows, plus the usual gifts, for a well-qualified woman."

Well, good luck. I'm going to water what's left of my garden. If there is any water."

"Ya, I haven't touched my scheme book yet. Are you going to the shop later?"

"Probably, see you there, Chafichu."

They went their separate ways: she up to the baboons and he down to the Ghetto.

iwe – you, informal used between friends and towards social subordinates

saka – therefore

rora - bride price – unlike European tradition where the woman brings the dowry, the Shona bridegroom gives gifts and a portion of his wealth to the bride's family, usually in the form of cows from his kraal.

Chapter 4   The Trekker

The universe can change within ten kilometers. Even in the space of a few meters, separate realities exist. To leave Happy Valley Farm and enter Chisungo Communal Lands was such a transition. To the unwary pilgrim crossing over was like perching on the crack of doom. Despite the purpose of the quest, illumination was often unplanned and unwelcomed.

The trekker, or nomad, didn't even know that he was to become such in due course. For the master of Happy Valley Farm lived blissfully unaware of the above differences with his gracious wife Betty and two faithful canine monsters: a German shepherd named Fritz and a Russian wolfhound called Tsar. Three married children and their broods had decamped to the safety of various cities during the war. Now that peace was four years old, white and black politicians settled into a predictable routine of arguing and collecting taxes. Hence the trekker liked to think he was safe above the eddies and currents of history.

Yet the current tranquility of Mathias Paul Van der Merwe was about to be rudely disturbed. In recent years, business often took him over the boundary. Especially after the war, these visits became more frequent as Van der Merwe's expertise in cattle farming was sought after by the new district government and various foreign-backed agencies. However, one particular journey was to become that single incident which would plunge him into the crevice of chaos which at the time seemed pure brimstone, but in the long run became the forge of recreation.

Mat ruled his fields and workers from the majestic vantage of a red Massey Ferguson tractor. He was fifty-two, had thin, red hair freckled with grey. His beardless ruddy face identified Mathias as a member of the beef and brandy tribe. Though an ample gut hung over the belt of his khaki shorts, his shoulders, arms and legs were knots of muscles from the demanding physical work which he wasn't ashamed to share with his laborers. He liked to take a walk on any evening through the sprouting maize fields to the rocky outcrop that guarded the long fertile valley which he inherited from his father and grandfather.

His sharp grey eyes looked right at a person without flinching or evading yet tiny crows' feet radiated laughter. Folks were frowning too much for their own good lately. Tom Drinkwater, a salty old mate, was apt to remind Mat: "This blerry kaffir country's drivin' us into the poor house. Goddamned Afs want to grab what don't belong to them."

Mathias considered his three thousand hectares of the richest dirt this side of Devuli Ranch and 750 head of the fattest cattle in the province. In fact, the local blacks called him *Murimi we Mombe*, the farmer of cows. Other assets included a rambling bungalow in the Cape Dutch style, a Renault 4 for the missus to pop into town for Saturday shopping, a trusty 1968 Kombi van without a speck of rust anywhere and a newer Ford truck. Over the years, Mat's chief mechanic, Rungamai Chitombo, made sure that his precious machinery: the tractor and the Kombi were in mint condition. Mat really did wonder at times what the hell Tom was frothing about. It was clear that the good Lord and the accommodating Shona were good to him. And as much as he would have liked to praise his good fortune, the persistent dead voice in his head would chide him away from a kind of happiness that he could have gloried in.

Hi grandfather, *Oopa*, the rugged trekker and

veteran of the war with the British, pulled his oxen team across the Limpopo River to rid himself of the English menace just ten years after the Boer War. His son Paul, a crueler replica of the old man, never let Matty forget that he was baas and he should bloody well act like it.

That was the ground of the farmer's identity. Yet as time went on that ground became increasingly shaky. For Mat was a victim of wealth and advantage. His approach to agriculture was not the questionable feudalistic traditions of his forebears but scientific because he went to *Gwebe* best agricultural school in the country. There his British instructors pounded into him the gospel of machinery and extensive cultivation. There was also an area buried by social convention which slept uneasily in his heart and that was friendship.

Because his mother died of black water fever when he was six months old, Mathias was breast fed and weaned by his nanny who was the mother of his only constant companion, Rungamai Chitombo. The two boys explored the bush with slings and curiosity. Old Pa was too busy carving out his empire in the veld to pay mind to his only son cavorting around all creation with the son of his nanny. European boarding school and wider white society put a stop to those golden days in the beetle buzzing grassland. Mat learned that he was superior and within a year his former playmate called him *kleinbaas*, little master. Gone were the names of *Jongwe* and Jesus. Jongwe was ChiShona for rooster depicting the flaming red mop belonging to Mat and Jesus was a loose translation of Rungamai's name into English.

Two things set Mathias apart from his fellow Afrikaners. Actually three: but it didn't do and it was too dangerous to admit the third. He spoke Shona like a Karanga peasant farmer courtesy of the Chitombo family and he mangled English like a proper East-end Londoner emulating a beloved teacher from high school and the BBC's "Coronation Street". And the years of growth, marriage and conformity forbade the consideration of the third: that nagging suspicion that he could happily reside in that other universe just around the corner. He assuaged this by rather progressive outpourings of charitable works as befitting a good member of the church of the Folk. The black man was his brother, but his junior brother.

The time came for Mathias to fulfil his Christian duty at Chose Mission. The minister of the church in town, Mr. Martin, was a man who believed in ecumenicalism even with black congregations. The superintendent of Chose Mission had invited Rev. Martin to guest preach at the next Sunday service. Unfortunately, he had a previous engagement so he called upon the respected elder Van der Merwe to take his place. The cattle farmer could not refuse, albeit with some reservations.

It proved to be a fine day as Mat started on his fateful trek. The wife was in Bulawayo at her Mum's so he had the trusty Kombi. Once past the Club – *folk said that it was going downhill lately, lettin' in all those uppity kaffirs as MEMBERS – past the mine turn off – there was another sore spot; blacks were working in the front office and no longer as sweepers either. No wonder the country was in a recession.*

The farmer's eye acutely perused the countryside. He nattered at the unresponsive scene. *Now didn't I tell them ignoramuses not to plant their bleedin' mealies on a hillside? Tch, and that mad carpenter still has his rondavel right at the crest of a hill so his kids will*

rondavel – round house, mud hut

50

get their deaths of cold this winter. Tch, fool!

Mathias knew the way: past a hopelessly overgrazed place called *Shwauka,* he was to look out for a big mountain and two cow signs. Turn right after the second cow sign at the big rock. The mountain was called *Msassa* and that was the entrance to Chose Mission. The Kombi screeched over the cattle grid which was really designed to keep out the people since the cows could nimbly step over the holes.

As the he sped down the single strip tarred lane, which was the behest of successive white governments, children and beasts scattered for safety. Matty good naturedly waved out the window. The kids stared and a few Sunday morning drinkers at the bottle store grumbled. "Ya, the white man rules forever."

Past a few Blair toilets which had chimneys where flies could escape, a few compounds with a sad lack of stock feed, some barren fields and the dilapidated students' dormitories came in sight. Matty always wondered why his church's schools looked so run down compared to the Catholic missions.

Since the Van der Merwes worshipped at the church in town, meeting the black reverend for the first time gave him a start. This man was not going to scrape and bow and say "yes or no, baas". The mouth smiled yet knew enough not to take the Boer's hand. And the eyes told Mat the truth, *what are you doing here, no-knees? As a Christian, I must tolerate you as a person must tolerate the heat. I loathe extending the smallest courtesies that I would even give to a white stranger. Finish your business and go away.*

Van der Merwe squeezed his bible like a shotgun and squeezed the leather. They walked into the side door

51

of the weather-stained and rusty-roofed church.

Hundreds of black faces peered up at the white man in the polished mahogany pulpit. A few teachers and local deacons sat in comfortable chairs at the side while the rest squeezed themselves onto poured cement benches. The inside walls hadn't been painted in ten years. Strong smells of ration meat, maize porridge, Sunlight soap and sweat afflicted his nostrils. *Oopa* boomed triumphantly in his head, *See, Matty, these kaffirs can't even wash for church!*

There had been no rain in Dhuma's village for six weeks and it was in the middle of the rainy season. Mat really thought that he was now facing his nemeses, but that was to come later. On cue the women rose and began to beat the drums and shake the calabashes giving the hymns a beautifully rhythmic cadence that their European composers would have envied.

Though his feet tapped to the rhythm, Mat's brain said, *it is lovely. But perhaps these heathen drums can be replaced by an organ.*

He spoke on Mark Chapter Three where Jesus told the crowds that whoever does the will of the Father were his mothers and brothers. Of course, Mat knew what that meant. *Did these people even begin to understand that he was their elder brother and that they should be grateful?*

Oopa chimed in, *hey some sneaking CIO spy may have slid in here just to cart you off to a porridge holiday at WaWa Prison. You watch your comments, son.*

CIO - national security police

After the service, as custom dictated, the station superintendent reluctantly invited his guest to lunch. Mat delicately declined. He had a bet going with Tom on the outcome of the game between Caps United and Lowveld Rangers and he wasn't going to miss that grudge match for nothing.

As he walked to the Kombi, he noticed a pea-sized house. *Must be he Af caretaker's place.* The outside bathroom and the bush fence around the garden confirmed his suspicions. Then a short white woman in red track pants and matching rubber thongs came out of the house. She had tucked her blonde hair under a head kerchief and her t-shirt pled for basic literacy – "If you can read this, thank a teacher." Hoe in hand, she meandered to the garden and began to cultivate grey pig manure into healthy tomato plants. Van der Merwe's attention was piqued. She sang a rock tune evidently enjoying herself. He noted that she had been absent from church, not that he expected any white people to actually live out here.

Then a short muscular man strolled into the enclosure as if he were welcome. Mat recognized him as one of the teachers he had picked up the previous Sunday. Giving lifts to local blacks was more a gesture to maintain good will for his business rather than friendship.

The woman and the man greeted each other in familiar *ChiShona* like old friends.

"*Mangwanani*, Chafichu, there's beer in the fridge," she said in what Mat thought to be a flat American accent.

mangwanani - good morning

53

"*Mamuka here, shanwari*, Let Ian Organize Nothing."

They both laughed and she queried, "Now how do you know I have Lion?"

"I have visions of at least a dozen very cold ones suffering from loneliness. I come to keep them company." He winked. They laughed again as he walked into the house. She remained in the garden. Ten seconds later Bob Marley's 'Zion Train' beat away the Sunday quiet.

A rage so virulent that it threatened to explode boiled up in the Boer. It was the anger at one of his people who had not kept up the side, had broken the rules of white decorum. Oopa supplied the ammunition. *The slut must be sleeping with every ningi who'll have her.*

Disgusted, Mat tromped down on the clutch and the accelerator. He ground the tired gears into reverse and plopped the van into a rut. An ominous hiss competed with the reggae for supremacy over the Sabbath calm. Frustrated, the Boer saw flashes of red. He leapt out of the van, went to the scene of disaster and lost control.

"Bloody, fucking slut!"

The shouting brought the white woman and her African friend out to see a scarlet-faced lunatic in a black suit simultaneously kicking a flat tire and pounding the side with a thick leather bible. Timorously she advanced and waited for this maniac to finish his episode.

mamuka here, shanwari – morning, pal

ningi – disreputable person, a nothing

"Sorry to bother you," typical Canadian effacement which he did not hear let alone understand. "Are you okay?"

Van der Merwe glared at her. She girded her loins for trouble like a nervous herd boy who advances toward a charging bull.

"Look mister, yer in trouble. I have a car and I can help you get your puncture fixed."

Her brusque tone simmered him down. He knew that his spare was being retreaded. He needed someone's help. Mat had never felt so helpless in the middle of foreign territory before.

She smiled reassuringly and said, "Well yer Kombi isn't gonna run away. Come in and have a cool drink. My name is Debbie Goerzen from Canada in case you're wondering." She held out her hand. Though misguided and probably jaded, she was still one of his people.

He took her hand and said, "Thank you. I'm Mathias Van der Merwe and I have a farm a bit west of here." He smiled lamely, a little ashamed that she had seen his tantrum.

The cooler living room also served as a dinette and study. Maps of Canada and Zimbabwe hung on the walls. Stacks of exercise books were piled up along the floor and cloth bound volumes filled the shelves. Two other Africans were lounging on the sofa. Matty's amicable mood instantly turned sour in that Jekyll-Hyde schizophrenic shift characteristic of most Rhodesians. He curtly nodded at the people in the room. "The one *munt* must have let in the others to steal the place blind." Oopa leered.

The concept that these men and this woman were colleagues still eluded him. Van der Merwe accidentally stumbled into the other universe. She wisely led him to an easy chair as she knew that he would not sit on the sofa, though there was room.

"It's hot out. Would you like a beer?" He decided that the best policy was to be polite and then rapidly leave.

"Thank you, no. It is the Sabbath."

She chuckled, "Is it really?" He was horrified at her seeming blasphemy. "Actually, Jesus was an Essene rabbi who celebrated the holy day on Wednesdays." She again laughed, this time at her own arcane joke. No one else thought it was very funny. "Well it's a rest from marking anyway." At this the rest of the group agreed. The trekker didn't know what they were talking about. "I do have some orange squash," she offered.

"Well it is hot. Do you have any Black Label?" He relented.

"Of course." She said.

As he sipped, the woman and the men carried on with their conversation, tacitly ignoring him. It became apparent that they were teachers. To fill in time, Mat decided to ask some questions. The rest fell silent watching.

"Excuse me, Miss Goerzen you teach here?"

"Yes." She was not going to make this easy for him, not at all.

"Are you in administration here?"

56

"Gawd no, I don't want grey hairs at my age."

"Well, you must be a head of department?" He was getting desperate.

"No."

Mathias could not conceive that a white could willingly work under a black. While he chatted, Manasseh began to clench and unclench his hands. Kindo began leafing through a magazine. Debbie was their friend and they didn't want to embarrass her by leaving. But soon they would have no choice if she didn't get rid of this fat monkey. Chafichu took the obvious hint which was lost on the Boer.

"Ah, Debbie, I need a glass from the kitchen."

"Sure, go head." Then she caught his eye. "I think I better go and clean some. They're all dirty."

In the kitchen Chafichu turned on her. "Debbie, get rid of this man. He is a bastard." His face was a thunderhead.

"How was I to know that he'd be such a creep? Imagine giving me a hassle about drinking beer in MY OWN house. And then the moron sips himself!"

"Why did you bring him inside? These Europeans are always rude."

"Listen, he was stuck. I'm not going to leave him there beating up his van."

"All right, I agree with that one." He recalled near lethal encounters with out of control Rhodesians and Chafichu did not want to be near any repeat performances. "But these Rhodesians will never get used to mixing with us."

"I just thought it would be okay," her face crumpled.

"It will never be all right," he raged in a whisper.

She knew she wasn't Jesus come to save the sinners. She could never heal the wounds of the Shona: an otherwise hospitable and open-handed people. That would take generations.

As they returned to the sitting room, Kindo and Manasseh were excitedly jabbering about local sports while Mathias morphed into a rainbow-colored piece of plywood sitting bolt upright in his chair. He visibly relaxed when she entered the room. Undeterred, he continued.

"Then you're a missionary?" He noted the German or Dutch sounding surname: Goerzen. Mathias didn't know about Canadian Mennonites, let alone half Ukrainian ones.

"Oh no, I'm a development worker but you can call me a contract teacher."

"You mean to tell me you left Canada to come here? Whatever for?"

"Why not?"

"How do these children learn?"

"Same as anywhere. You get your dummies your averages and your geniuses. And we have a few of them at this school."

"You mean dummies?"

Chafichu was just about to hit him.

"No, geniuses," she countered. "Plus, the majority of average students. One thing though, these kids care more about learning something than the spoiled brats at home. Maybe it's because the people fought for the right to put their kids into the classroom." She looked hard at the Boer.

Mat frowned into his beer. He had the feeling that this woman was not going to take him aside and tell him how terrible it really was. She was clearly having a good time with her friends. She began to introduce the other teachers and he nodded. "These are my comrades in crime," she announced expansively.

The trekker felt as if he were sinking into a slime pit. *This is not the way it is supposed to be!* He winced on the word comrade. *She must be one of those communists,* he thought. The company turned to other topics ignoring him because he had nothing more to say. It was almost too much that he was in the same room.

Honesty was too ingrained in him to ignore what his eyes saw. Consequently, Mathias flailed for his life grabbing at a non-existent lifeline. Even Oopa, the nagging alter ego, deserted him. This would be the closest thing that Van der Merwe had ever come to a hallucinogenic experience. It wouldn't be his last, however. He was taught that when blacks and whites shared beer, Armageddon drew near.

"Mr. Van der Merwe, why don't we take your tire down to Mr. Ruka's? He'll fix it good for you."

Driving to his lily-white bungalow later that afternoon, Mathias felt that he had narrowly slipped through of the devil's clutches. But he had not really

59

escaped. From now on doubt would nip at his heels. The scenario in that house was almost unfathomable. He was sure that two of those lads were spies and gunrunners for the terrorists in the war and that one in the beret: some nasty memory was triggered. *Wasn't he a bloody terrorist?* But the Africans hinted at nothing. They had taken off his tire and got it fixed for only two dollars. Mat was sure it was going to blow again. But there had been no trouble and he was already at the Club turn off. Matty needed liquid succor because the hysterical voice of Oopa continued the usual recriminations in his head.

Chapter 5   The Club

The experience whined in his ears like an air raid siren. Cheeks flushed, hear pounding, hands sweating on the steering wheel, Mat was angry, confused and thirsty. The Club's entrance blurred ahead of him. It was safe ground with his people, a return to balance.

The metal door of the bar was open. A friendly glow shone from the red shaded lamps through the wrought iron lattice work that protected their den from non-members. Mathias, who wanted to slink in unnoticed, was loudly accosted by his old neighbor and drinking partner.

"Well, Matty, ya old soak. Yer in yer Sunday best. Come and buy me a bloody drink." Tom Drinkwater, anchored by his glass, perched precariously on his stool. About the same age as Mat, Tom was soft and flabby where the Boer was muscular. A pair of thick, brown, horn rimmed glasses kept sliding down Tom's fleshy nose. His accent, a constant assault on any long vowel sound, made the farmer's Afrikaner English sound patrician.

"Josh, give Mr. Drinkwater what he wants and a double brandy for me." Van der Merwe slumped on his stool, loosened his tie and catatonically stared at the till. Silently Joshua Dube, *Baba* Tavonga, chemist, stock clerk and unacknowledged Club psychiatrist, landed the brandy near Matty's waiting grasp.

"Hey Matty, ya look like the time the terrs burnt yer barn and carried off your prize Brahmin heifer." Tom's victim flinched and moved his smoldering eyes toward the flabby Drinkwater. Old Tom usually conducted church service as soon as the bar opened at 10 a.m.

Is this all he could come up with after three hours of Sabbath contemplation? Mathias thought nastily. "*Nya*, Tom. It ain't me blerry mombes this time."

"Here now, Mat, I thought you'd be snuggled nicely with a pint watchin' the match. Where were you?"

"At a church in the TTL east of here."

"Oh, at a bloody Af rally," Drinkwater chuckled.

"*Nya,* a service."

"Well, what the hell, yer goin' soft on me, mate?"

Matty's stared at the chilly solace of till and bottles. Metal and glass, bodies and ideas could be smashed, crushed, blown up, disintegrated. He was a farmer. *He knew viscerally that land was the only thing that couldn't be destroyed. It could erode, desiccate or flood. Humans lived and died on it, fought and loved on it, cried and prayed to it. But it remained in some form – silent observant. He felt that it did not matter who owned land; it belonged to itself – omnipotent and everlasting.*

"I was preachin'."

"Huh?" Bleary Tom leered at Van der Merwe. "Savin' their souls, eh? Ja, but you speak their lingo, don't ya?"

"It's useful," Matty snapped, "to know what yer enemy is talkin' about."

Joshua Dube, *Baba* Tavonga, rearranged glasses listening intently. *This old man was going mad. Why?*

nya – no – Afrikaans

Van der Merwe leaned over and said semi-audibly. "Ye know the Afs say that we are hard core Boers and we'll never change short of the power of God." He remembered what the young woman had told him as he started his Kombi.

"You know, Mr. Van der Merwe, when I was in South Africa, I met Boers who had changed their minds. Some Afrikaners like Beyers Naude no longer believe in the superiority of the white race and some even go to jail because they support African rights."

Traitors! He thought immediately. *Nothing short of the power of God!* Mat leafed through his memories and recalled: *I am the God of wars. The governments of the world are laid down by My hand.* Did that include those ZANU PF chaps who sat in their nice parliament building on the corner of Third and Baker in Salisbury?

No, Mat really didn't like Tom Drinkwater and his blasphemous statements. Even the Afs had more respect for God. But Mathias, as Oopa was never remiss in reminding him, came from a long line of trekkers, nomadic cattle herders who wandered over the veld of Southern Africa until the exodus to Transvaal to protect a Way of Life. Forgetting the Leviticus dictum that a slave could only be owned for seven years, his family enslaved Africans for generations. Everybody did. And those interfering British tried to stop things with their 'we know what's best for everyone' policy. Oopa fought the Brits in 1900 and ended up in a concentration camp. The Boers were forced to live no better than their former bondsmen. Then in wagons loaded with everything they owned, his family headed north on their last trek across the muddy Limpopo River.

Mathias was born in a pleasant green valley with

two rivers flowing through it. His father named it Happy Valley and the name stuck. Mat was a child of freedom which was wrested from the six villages of the *Majira* clan who were resettled on the rocky hills of southern Gutu. He didn't know about this until the war when the terrs and told his workers to seize the farm for the Majira Clan. Mat thought this was the biggest joke of the war until one night his old nanny, Ambuya Chitombo, came to his house.

Mathias was having supper with Betty in the kitchen. His FN 3 was stashed under a chair. A soft knock on the back door...

"Terrs!" He stiffened in his seat.

"Mat, control yourself until you know who it is. I swear old man, you're going to have a heart attack and then what am I going to do?"

Betty went to the door. "Ach, it's only Ambuya Chitombo."

Mathias got up and went out on the back veranda. "What do you want, Ambuya?"

"Excuse me, Madam and Baas. I am sent." Always respectful, she looked at her calloused toes.

"By who?" He queried.

"You know. They say that the soldiers are going to attack this place. But they also say that you and the Madam are somehow good, especially the Madam. They do not want to kill you."

"So old woman, I'm supposed to pack up and leave my farm to get blown up?" Though he was very fond of Ambuya, he thought that this old dear was crossing the line into impudence.

"I am sorry Baas but you are having no choice. You and the Madam must come with me just for tonight.

Mathias was about to chase her away when he heard a safety mechanism being clicked off. She was not alone.

An hour later Mat, Betty and Ambuya were scrambling down into a hollow about three kilometers from the house. He was carrying their double sleeping bag and air mattresses which they used for camping in the national parks. Betty carried a flask of tea. In another hundred meters, they arrived at a deserted hut which looked as if it hadn't been used for twenty years yet the thatch was new and the walls were regularly repaired. Immediately Ambuya busied herself with kindling a small fire.

It was a chilly early July night and the blaze was welcome. However, Mat was worried that the fire might attract some unwelcome guests.

"Do not worry, Baas. The comrades will not attack a spirit medium's house and the soldiers do not know this place." The old woman seemed to read his thoughts.

"This is the *imba yanopiro* of my husband's people where they met the ancestors." The grandmother announced. Then in a chanting tone she recalled all the generations of Chitombos beginning with her husband and working backwards. Mathias counted thirty. That was impossible. The Africans came after the Boers. Even

imba yanopiro – house where a family speaks to the ancestors

Mat could proudly say that he sprang from fifteen generations of Afrikaners. She then went to a shelf in the back and reverently brought out a drinking vessel and bowl. In both gnarled hands, she presented the artifacts like a priest giving communion. The designs on the pottery were still strong but the dyes had faded with the centuries. Mat remembered his Geology. The clay was of local origin and it was old, very old.

"Chitombo's people were the soldiers of *Soro Rezhou* the first King of *Dzimbabwe* who chased the *San* into the desert. The son of Rezhou, who was ruling Dzimbabwe after, gave this land to the Majira clan for their good service. Before my husband died, he entrusted me with this knowledge in order to pass it on to his children." She spoke quietly and distinctly revealing a deep pride in her people's history.

After some time, she left them to pass the night peacefully. But Mathias tossed and turned for what remained of it. This war was too disturbing. Oh yes, there were the threats and deaths and bombs but something else was happening that unsettled him even more. Unwanted truths kept knocking at his genetically thick Dutch skull and his upbringing vied with his innate honesty for his soul. The Rhodesian Broadcasting Corporation lied over two media: radio and television. The war was not being won for White Christian Civilization. Chisungo Tribal Trust Land was a semi-liberated zone. Everything off the main road was closed: schools, clinics, post offices.

If the terrs were supposedly raping and killing everybody in the villages, why were twelve-year-old majiba spying and carrying food and guns to the terrs? Why didn't the rewards of money and bicycles attract more people to report on the guerrillas? And why, in God's name, were the people feeding the terrs even to the

66

extent of growing crops for this ragged army? Who was doing this? He had even heard that some white farmers openly supported the vakomana, the boys in the bush.

As for himself, he was neutral. Mat was sensible enough to know that if he actively went against the terrs, his farm would be destroyed. He loved the land too much to let politics get in the way, besides this war would end one day. Whichever way it turned out, he would still live in Chisungo District and he had to do business with the blacks who lived here: best not to make unnecessary enemies. And without labor he could not manage the farm.

Old Smitty's propaganda said that the blacks were inferior and they needed a LONG time to reach European standards, if ever. One couldn't depend on the backward rural black. From experience Mat knew this to be nonsense. Rungamai and Farai were the best mechanics he ever had.

Because of Farai's good English, Mat had promoted him to work in the house. The mechanic did not like cooking or ordering around the other servants. In frustration, he sabotaged a few inner parties and was promptly sent back to the workshop. On reflection, Mat could feel for Farai. They both loved engines and Mat would not want to cook for his wife's fancy 'progressive' friends either. He began to learn that it was not wise to treat a black man like a woman. He respected Farai and needed him in the workshop not the kitchen.

But Oopa was always ready to distract the Boer from coming to any helpful insights which stemmed from his experience.

Matty, yer goin' soft with this war. How can you respect a black baboon from copying what you

*showed him? Sure, they do all right at the mission
schools and there's thousands of 'em studyin' overseas.
But we taught them everything they know. They lived
like animals before we came. Don't be a bleedin'
kaffirboetie. You know that it they win, they'll take
everything I fought for.*

There's no bloody way I'm leaving' this place!
Mat screamed at his ancestral voice. *And you didn't fight
for it. You took it. Or it was taken like our land was
taken by the English who shamed us. You think I'm goin'
back to South Africa!* His thoughts lowered in volume
and he mumbled to himself. *Besides, it's only a matter of
time when the blacks will rise up there too and then
where will I go to at my age? Oopa, you know you can't
keep what you take by force. Look at the Brits. They
tried to destroy us. But who's rulin' South Africa now:
The Nationalist Party, good old verechte Boers. Logic
tells me that it's the same with the Afs. You can't keep
them poor and stupid in the TTLs forever. Even Old
Smitty said we should educate them eventually. But it
seems they've educated themselves, maybe with a little
help from those Commie chaps – what the hell am I doin'
talkin' such rubbish to ghosts.*

With that final thought, he managed to clear his
brain of any rambling and concentrate on the brooding
silence of the ebony night. Just he and Betty were at the
farm now with the workers and the terrs – vakomana –
comrades? Dawn began to pale the stars when he finally
fell asleep curled up against his woman in their double
sleeping bag.

"Mat, Mat." His wife was shaking him awake.
For a moment, he thought he was in his own bed.

kaffirboetie – little brother of the African, race traitor

verechte – righteous, proper

"Ja, that's all right. Cephas can git the chaps to bring the planter out of the barn. Good God!" He looked up and saw the rafters jointing the thatch of the hut. "Oh yeah, I forgot."

"Ambuya Chitombo has been here. We can go home now." Betty said gently.

He was very frightened by what the sunrise would reveal. Had they lost everything? Climbing up the hill to the farmyard, black flakes from the burnt-out barn were carried by the wind. "Oh shit," he moaned. Betty squeezed his arm.

A fetid wind blew off the land. A bovine corpse with its legs cut off greeted the pair as they opened the gate. Its bones sticking out of the thorax had fouled the air. Betty stated it first to ease the pain. "Oh dear, it's your prize heifer." Mathias groaned. "Maybe they were hungry," she said.

On closer inspection of the barn, Mat found that miraculously the planter had been saved. The tractor and the other equipment had the kind of damage that could be fixed with hard work but they could be repaired. Then his foot scraped against a mortar shell in the dirt. To his dismay a Rhodesian army stamp was on the casing. "Bloody stupid bastards can't aim properly."

The house was still standing but it was a mess. A battle had taken place there the whole night. But the broken windows, cracked doors and perforated roof could also be fixed. Mat was stubborn optimist. He went around to the front and across the road he could see his fields freshly dry ploughed and he thought about the corpse of his cow. It could very well have been him and Betty. He was humbly thankful that they had been

69

spared. Within a week, Mrs. Van der Merwe continued to feed the Boys in the Bush.

War torn, rotting bodies riddled by hatred turned into manure and smelled of new growth. Something powerful and frightening germinated in the soil. It was scarred but strong from its violent breech birth. It would multiply sixty to one hundredfold. This was the new nation. What did they call it? Zimbabwe: a big house of stone. This was the substance of his vision that morning when he looked at his fields. Then he turned away from its imminence and its inevitability. He and his kind would continue to hole up in their clubs with signs that read RIGHT OF ADMISSION RESERVED. He would continue to play bowls on courts guarded by the notice WHITES ONLY.

Yet it was predestined for this trekker to make a pilgrimage, *mbunu ane rwendo kunopira*, the Boer would make a spiritual journey, unwanted and unprepared, yet as obvious as the coming of the new nation. In his lifetime, Mathias would see the withering of the Rhodesian Way of Life. History had found him and he was distressed. Those white people who joined with the Africans to march on this new path crashed through the fields of his security trampling hard on his roots until he felt weak just thinking about it.

Sunk in the slough of his past, Mat glumly drank off his third double brandy and ordered another one. It was hard to change at fifty-two. How did thought become action? How indeed did a man bear the fruits that befitted repentance?

The long silence disturbed Tom. "Jesus, man, you're unhinged!"

"Maybe, maybe not." Mat replied softly, still half way between worlds.

"What the hell happened out there?"

"I gave a sermon to the lot 'bout knowin' their own place," he answered bitterly. "After," he paused, "I met a Canadian. You know she teaches the blacks and she actually enjoys it. Got me in a room full of those *munts*. Now I been in rooms full of 'em before but this wasn't the same. We were all equal like." His voice thudded to a whisper on the second last word. His comment had meant to exorcise the spell that Debbie Goerzen's living room had on him.

As usual Tom heard only what he wanted to hear. "Ha, Canadians," Tom sneered. "You know what they are."

"Ja," Mat affirmed.

"A bunch of kaffirboetie, commies and dirty Danes screwin' every munt who'll have 'em."

This litany of self- justification made Van der Merwe feels a bit easier because he didn't have the strength or the inclination to do anything except to join in, "Ja, Russian spies really. We were doin' fine till these foreigners came to stir up the pot."

"Shit man, don't give 'em that much credit. They're from fucking Mars!"

Joshua Dube cleaned glasses. He liked Martians. *This Canadian woman was teaching his son, Tavonga, in form four. The boy reported that she was a good white. Baba Tavonga knew, however, that usually this goodness only lasted for about six months or so. And then these nice liberal Martians from the planet of Canada or Britain or the U.S. would come under the*

munts – Africans

spell of the Rhodesians. The expatriate's friendliness would turn to mere politeness and then to indifference. And miraculously, if the devil could perform miracles, a new Rhodesian would be created in Ian Smith's own image.

The trouble with this country, Joshua thought, *was that even the black man who others thought would go with the aspirations of his people, even the African had to struggle with a choice. And both whites and blacks had to confront the dilemma of Southern Africa: whose side are you on? For a white it was not as easy as one would think.*

Take a human being who hated apartheid when he came. Oh yes, Baba Tavonga had seen the fresh contract teachers trying to learn Shona in a bottle store, playing slug with the peasant farmers, calling Africans comrade. In a year's time or even six months that human being who happened to be white would instead play bowls at the Club, go to the theater in town, only visit other white teachers or Rhodies and they would exchange Shona for *Chilapalapa* the slangy argot of the South African mines. These white strangers made friends with unrighteous mammon: the exquisite dinner parties featuring salmon and South African wine, the trips to the *bundu* in borrowed land rovers, the almost irresistible and illegal foreign currency deals. All this enamored many expatriates to the Rhodesian Way of Life. Materially the African wasn't even in the running. Besides unreserved hospitality, as tradition dictated, the only things that the Africans could offer a white stranger were their complete and loyal friendship, and the participation in their ancient culture. Blacks could only offer a share in the changing of the seasons, in grief and in joy. For many this was far too little.

bundu - bush

72

Baba Tavonga continued to muse while he mechanically served the customers. *Especially for many black brothers and sisters, this was far too little. They wanted what the whites had for ninety years: money and power.* He didn't blame them for that.

Money and power are all right but add to that greed and the class system and that equals the destruction of African culture: or any culture for that matter. And this was one thing that Joshua wanted to protect and nurture as his fathers had done before him because he was an *n'anga,* a traditional healer. From as far away as northern Gutu and southern *Nyaunde* people came to his compound for treatment and consolation.

Yet this Goerzen woman did not change toward him and the others who worked at the Club. She was still happy at Chose Secondary and she made friends with the black members of the club, very promising. But Mr. Dube was afraid that sensible Boers like Van der Merwe would influence her with his rationality. Then again, Murimi we Mombe was acting very strange lately. Ah, it is the hot drinks. He drank five double tots already.

Wearing a Euripidean smile, Joshua beamed at the two reeling whites. "Another drink, Sirs?" He had watched the *marungu* get disgustingly drunk for the last fifteen years. *Is this the trade off,* he thought, *Am I just another mutengesi, sell out? No,* he reminded himself. *The comrades drank a lot of booze and ate a lot of meat from this place.* He had done his part. Also, this job paid for school fees for his four children and a house girl for his wife. He endured it.

***   ***   ***

The next Friday afternoon Mat drove east along the highway and turned down a dust road leading to

Chisungo Office the administrative post snuggled in the lap of wooded hills. Just past the newly painted rural hospital, Matty had to brake hard around a bend because a rusty five ton white Nissan truck blocked the way. A small crowd of black youths were slowly pushing the heavy vehicle off the road while two bearded men, one tall and one short wearing a black beret shouted directions. Mat recognized the adults as two of the of the chaps who sat in that Canadian woman's sitting room.

Boer pulled up behind. Immediately Kindo, whose green three-piece suit was caked with red dust, ran up alongside the farmer's Ford truck. Unseen Kudakwashe strolled over to the other side of the cab. Matty looked from one to the other as Kindo hurriedly chronicled their most recent disaster.

"Good afternoon, Mr. Van der Merwe," Kudakwashe said distinctly.

"Ja, good day to you." Recognition lit the Boer's face. "You're Kudakwashe Chitombo, ain't ya?" A gentleness he secretly reserved for anyone in the Chitombo family moderated the Boer's approach. He considered helping the group.

"That's right. I happen to be the sports master on this ill-fated mission."

Matty glanced at the youngsters who looked very disappointed. "Ja, I see you're in trouble here. What's wrong with the truck?"

"Ah, no spare tire. The mission insists on dealing with those crooks who buy from South Africa instead of Botswana. So, we have to suffer."

A little miffed, Mat queried," Now who's in

charge of this Tom Foolery?"

"Your friend Rev. Mapfumo," Kuda answered quietly.

Matt grumbled. There was something amiss in the administration of his church's schools. This was not the first incident that he knew of. And these kids were going to miss their game because of it. "Which school were you going to?"

"Just down the road to Tagona Secondary, just six ks from here."

The Boer saw the dismay of the students replaced by a glimmer of hope. He remembered that these same men helped him out of his own recent mess. He asked, "How many boys need a lift?"

"There are just ten boys and three of us."

"Ach, that'll be no problem. Two of you chaps git in the front with me and I'm sure this old girl can fit eleven in the back."

Kindo's clapped his hands effusively. He practically groveled, "Oh thank you, Chef. God bless you!"

Kuda put his hands in his trouser pockets and looked the Boer in the eye. "Are you sure, Mr. Van der Merwe?"

"Bloody, sure. I was just going by there anyway."

"Of course, the school will pay you for your petrol."

"Nya, don't worry about that unless I have to bring you back. I'm just going over to the DA's to pick up some Agritex scouting forms. Then I can come and check you at the match."

"Are you sure that you've got nothing else to do?" Kuda insisted.

"No no. What else is there to do except go home and watch my mombes keel over?"

Kuda could now afford to smile. "Very good. You won't regret this, chef."

"Well, let's not waste any more time."

Meanwhile Chafichu stood in front of the bonnet with his arms folded observing the interplay. He relayed the message to the boys who cheered and whistled. Each boy clapped hands and thanked Matty as he passed by the cab. Kuda and Kindo climbed into the front while Tawanda silently got into the back. He brooded for the rest of the journey.

Later that evening, Mat quietly closed the screen door on his own veranda. "I'm home, Luv." He smiled in the darkness at his trim grey-haired wife who serenely knitted a pair of pink baby booties.

"So, Matty, you finally remember where you live," she taunted in good humor.

He eyed the dainty wool in anticipation. "Well which of the girls is in the family way now?"

"Rachel called today from *Kadoma* with the good news."

Mat took off his hat and sat in the low cane bottomed rocker beside Betty. "Good on us, old girl. Looks like the clan is increasing. When's she due?"

"Around the end of July." Betty smelled the beer on her husband. Not in an accusing way did she ask him. Theirs was a happy marriage with mutual trust. She seldom begrudged Matty his drink because he worked hard and was a good husband to her. "Who was at the Club tonight?"

"I wasn't there." In a faraway voice and bemused gaze, he continued. "I was having' a few pints at a teacher's house at Chose Mission."

In the dim light thrown off by the yellow 40-watt bulb, she looked quizzically at his preoccupied expression. "How did you end up there?" Betty was curious and urged more details from him. She was intrigued and pleased with the changes that were beginning to take place in her husband.

"Well, as you know I was on my way to pick up them stock scouting forms from the DA's office when I saw the Chose truck stuck in the middle of the road.

"Those poor kids looked so down in the mouth. And I remembered that these same African chaps, who didn't even like me, helped me with the flat tire on Sunday. So I drove the whole lot to their game. And oh my, those kids were superb. They ran like gemsbok, just beautiful. It was a very good match and you know I don't say a thing like that lightly.

"Well the next thing you know, I'm drivin' the kids back to the school and they're singing all the way. The African teachers invited me to drink a few."

"Sounds interesting. What did you think of these teachers?"

"Very intelligent crew. I can see why Chitombo is pleased as punch with his boy, Kudakwashe. Gawd Luv, we must be getting on. I recall him as a dusty little pickanin. And it was tough at the time to agree to send Chitombo's kids to school."

"That's why I married you, Mat." She remembered a dance in Salisbury over 30 years ago when she and a couple of silly college girlfriends went on a hunting expedition to snag rich boyfriends. She saw a muscular, red-haired chap regaling his mates about a wrestling match he had won at the Gwebe College sports day. *Oh God, another thuggish farmer*, she thought.

Then he looked at her and smiled. She swam in his grey blue eyes. That was the beginning and three decades, three children and two grandchildren later, Betty Walker still loved what she found to be an honest, generous and kind man. She saw how he talked to his workers not in the clipped and curt Chilapalapa but in the musical ChiKaranga that she would soon learn. She also knew that he paid his laborers government wages plus the regulation annual wage increase. Matty did play favorites to some extent; he paid particular solicitude to the senior house maid Mrs. Chitombo, whom he called Ambuya. Betty smiled at her husband as he continued his long-winded tale.

"In the long run, it worked out fine. Kuda is this big bearded man with his own sons. He was very responsible with the way he handled those students. Ya know I haven't seen much of Rungamai since he decided to open up his own shop the end of the war.

"Then there was this well dressed good looking

character named Kindo. I don't think that's his real name. He was quite silly but I think it's an act like it is with most clowns.

"Finally, there was this short, very tough, clever chap named Tawanda Murovi. He asked me a lot of hard questions about what I thought of Zimbabwe. But I was seated in his sitting room and he kept plying beer on me.

"I must say that I spent a much better evening than listening to Tom and Fred bitch about everything. You know, I'm comin' to think that with clever honest men like the Africans I met, this country's going to be all right."

Betty smiled broadly. She said pensively. "You know Mat, we've lived here all our lives and yet we've been so blind. The beauty of this land isn't in the exotic wild animals; it's in the people."

"Ja," he replied, "During the war I was afraid that a black government would strip us of everything. But that hasn't happened yet. And I hope to Christ it never does."

"Well the war is finished and we have lost nothing. It's good to see that things are improving for the blacks. In fact, we have gained because we don't have to be afraid to make the friends we want, go where we want and think the way we want," she said.

"You always were ahead of me on these types of things." He squeezed her hand.

"Are you hungry?"

"Nya, let's turn in," he whispered.

She pulled him into the dark house.

79

Chapter 6   Chafichu's Last Stand

Between sunrise and breakfast the establishment sleeps. The interior is never impressive unless one is intrigued by the ultra-decadent. A sagging cement counter with peeling paint, equally sagging shelves like an old crone's pendulous breasts, dusty bottles, last night's bottle caps and gritty, white plastic Chibuku pails greet the bleary-brained patron. A temperamental stereo is essential to any bottle store however humble. Lack of even Radio Three over a ghetto blaster can bankrupt any business. A smashed window lends the joint character for there is a colorful history behind each crack.

How is the typical bottle store more than a fetid beer hole fit only for thugs and whores? People. It is the complete abandonment of cares and worries to either vice or joy: pure laughter and pure dance. Often, however, a boozy reminder of those cares blazes into the usual shouting match leading to a five-hour debate ending in blows and embraces.

In recent years, this one hundred percent home grown institution has become controversial: has even become the subject of parliamentary debate. According to its detractors, the bottle store is a despicable dive and a corrupter of youth. However, the township and village locals do have their apologists who uphold the bottle store as the firm bastions of democracy in a hierarchical and status-ridden society.

That night from Mai Nyasha's place in Dhuma's village Chafichu, Kuda, the Chef Urozvi, Debbie and Johnny emerged. On their way to the headmaster's car, they could still hear the funkier than usual rhumba beat.

Inside they could still see the wobbly steel tables with peeling sky blue paint. These were actually disguised launch pads for the late flight of drunken patrons. As the local *chidakwa* slid, thunked and dissolved onto the floor, often with a beatific smile, the bouncer would adroitly swing into action. Mai Nyasha's retainer Jervis the Kung Fu Master would lift the body over the assortment of tables, benches and beer crates where dazed customers reclined with their ladies for the night.

Here at Mai Nyasha's, discreetly beyond the mission boundary and legally a member of the Chief's kraal, everybody knew everybody else's business. The bartender wore a disco t-shirt instead of the regulation white shirt and black tie found in the town bars. Meanwhile, Jervis carried the obstacle off the premises. As the drunkard's neighbors led him home bleating for just one more liter of liquid porridge, a hot slug game was in progress.

At this point the Choselites left this haven of blue-lit noise. They entered the Chef's Peugeot 404 station wagon with the drunken temerity of fools and headed for the Club. Going from a pulsating moon-lit night to a dreary sunless morning, the company cautiously strolled over the threshold bearing the Members Only sign. Chafichu chimed a little too loudly.

"A member of what: The Human Race?" He chuckled self-satisfied, "*Iri*, fine. I can get into this place."

COUNTDOWN TO COMBAT

Kuda steered Chafichu and the others to an unoccupied table near the dart boards. Debbie, Johnny

chidakwa – drunkard   *iri* – ok

81

and the Chef went to the bar to sign in their fellow *gandangas* and buy the first round.

Meanwhile the seated Choselites anxiously peered out of the corner of their eyes like castaways in a mine field. The fool saint regulars jealously guarded their stations at the bar. Tom challenged Matty to a game of darts. As they finished their drinks and ordered another round, Tom continued his story.

"Then this smart lookin' kaffir comes into the front office and says that he's from the ministry of labor." He demonstrated his point by pushing the air currents with his hand. Mat ignored him and greeted the newcomers.

Tom frowned and said, "Well come on, mate. Let's play the best of three for a round."

Chafichu leaned on the arm of Johnny's chair. He warily watched the two whites approach the dart board.

10 – 9 – 8

"Hey blas, look at those stupid looking *mabunu* with the big stomachs." Chafichu winked at Kuda.

Chitombo joined the conspiracy. "Which one, they're both stupid with big guts."

"The one with the specs, the other is our perhaps soon-to-be-comrade Murimi. The other one is a bastard."

Johnny's natural caution sensed all the danger signals of a brewing fight. Debbie just joined the table as

gandanga - thug

82

Johnny moaned, "Ah. Tawanda, leave him alone."

"I am not doing anything. I just gave a comment."

"Yeah, comments like that always get you into fights. Besides, I don't feel like protecting you from the bad guys tonight."

"Or any other night, it seems. But I do not want to fight. It's just that I cannot stand to look at that Boer who had fun when he killed many many majiba. Also, you never lived under their regime. They were horrible. Our people say that if you kill too many men, you go mad."

"You know Comrade Grenade?"

"I've heard of him."

"Ah, that guy. He would go against a whole stick of soldiers just him and his bazooka. He was a serious warrior, that one. His village is near my home and my relatives say that he just drinks his demobilization pay and begs for more beer. Otherwise he sits."

"That's terrible," Johnny exclaimed, "Isn't the government doing anything for him?"

"What can they do? He was in the army after independence. But he got drunk on duty one night and shot the leg of one of his privates. Very awkward. That's why they had to chuck him out."

"Now what does Grenade have to do with Drinkwater?"

"They got the same problem. This." And he tapped his half full pint of Lion.

Tawanda continued. "My cousin works at the mine and he says that Drinkwater is even drunk at work. If he were an African, he would have been chased from his job. But no, this place practices apartheid. He will never be sacked. That's why I cannot stand to look at him."

4 – 3 – 2

They were speaking in low whispers. The club did not have the same freewheeling democracy of a bottle store. At that moment, Drinkwater backed up to aim for a shot and he stumbled over Chafichu's straddled legs.

"Here, what's this? Git out of me way!" He scowled at Murovi. The look was not lost on the younger African and they exchanged fierce stares.

"I am not in your way." Murovi announced.

1 – IGNITION

"Who the hell are you, anyway? I said git."

Johnny nudged Chafichu. "Come on Tawanda, sit down. Kuda just left his chair."

"Why should I move in my own country?" Murovi shouted.

Mat tried to calm his friend down. "Come on, Tom. The kid's over a meter from the foul line."

"That's too fucking bad. This blerry Af is ruining my game." Then Tom stubbornly stepped on Chafichu's foot. "I said, git out of my way, you kaffir bastard," he intoned viciously.

Murovi was equally obstinate. "No!" His eyes speared Drinkwater and he was tempted to spit.

Tom's sense of drama increased with his blood pressure. "Hey," he shouted, "Who let this boy in here?"

At the bar, Chef Urozvi put his face in his hands and moaned, "oh, God."

Shock bolted the Canadians to their chairs. In the quiet few seconds that followed, the slow kindled valor of her people sparked in the woman. Like the Shona, Canadians seldom went to war. They were content to stay home and till their fields. But in the intricate stonework that was emerging Zimbabwe, even the stranger was forced to choose a side. This was the time for Debbie and Johnny.

Debbie Goerzen's people were the good farmers that Tsarina Katherine had brought from Germany to show the Russians how to do the job properly. There was one wrinkle; they were Mennonite and did not join in Russia's wars so eventually her family was also forced to trek to another place to find religious freedom.

She said. "This man is my colleague and I let him in."

Though Johnny actually signed in Chafichu, he didn't dare utter a word. John Macabe was powerless in the face of his chosen indecision.

Tom hissed at Debbie. "So git him out of here, *kaffirboetie*."

Mat stood between Drinkwater and Murovi who was now standing with his fists cocked. Then an inner clarity focused Murovi's vision and he saw Tom as a pitiful creature eaten away by hatred. Compassion and ancient tradition loosened Chafichu's hands.

He said quietly, "I'm sorry. I cannot hit an old man." He walked to the bar and sat by the Chef.

Maddened Drinkwater lunged after Murovi. Mat grabbed him, "Tom, Tom! Stop it! Go home, Tom. The war's been over for four years! Go home."

Mat held Drinkwater in a bear hug and half carried him out the door. In the time that it took the Choselites to take one last sip, they left the Club except for Johnny.

At the Club executive meeting the next week, it was announced that Tawanda Murovi, also known as Chafichu, was permanently banned from the Club as a guest. It was also demanded that Debbie Goerzen, a member of no longer good standing, apologize to Tom Drinkwater for the rude behavior of Murovi. Mathias Van der Merwe was the only executive member who dissented.

Chapter 7   Pay Day

Debbie refused to apologize to the likes of Tom Drinkwater. She was not surprised but disappointed by the unnecessarily dramatic outcome. Undeterred at month end, she and most of the teachers joined the routine convoy into town to cash pay cheques, buy groceries, have lunch and drink at the only fancy hotel in town. In fact, most civil servants from the rural areas descended on Masvingo's stores and bars with their modest wads of twenty dollar bills.

At the hotel, she was pleasantly surprised to see Bill Fox her old pal from the contract teacher orientation in Ottawa. His nickname was Wild Bill because apart from his esteemed grandfather Charlie Fox, Bill idolized Wild Bill Cody, buffalo hunter, cowboy and impresario. Where Cody was a bearded and blonde American, his acolyte Wild Bill II hailed from northern Ontario. He was tall, broad shouldered, and bronze skinned. He tied back his long dark hair.

"Hey Bill, long time no see," Debbie invited herself to the table he was sharing with an African colleague.

"Hi Deb, are the baboons still eating your garden?" He laughed.

"What garden, oh you mean my new Japanese rock and dirt garden?"

"Hey, how bad is the water situation at Chose?" Bill became serious.

"Not great. We're lucky to get two hours of water in our houses every day while the poor students have to survive on a bucket of water for washing and cleaning their clothes. But all the kids opted to stay. Even with the strict water rationing, they at least are eating decent meals three times a day. Their families at home can't guarantee that. How about you and your school?"

"About the same. Sorry, I'm being ignorant. I haven't introduced my buddy Cephas Kanjanga. He's my H O D, boss of the science department."

Debbie smiled as she shook Kanjanga's hand. He asked, "So how are you finding Zimbabwe?"

"I'm generally having a great time." She looked around the bar and said more quietly, "But it would be better if the all the Rhodie's *ivapoed* themselves to their beloved South Africa."

Cephas chuckled, "Sorry to disappoint you, but most of these Rhodesians are not qualified to do the big jobs in South Africa. *Saka*, we must endure them. Take Ian Smith for example. Many people wanted at least to see him imprisoned if not hanged. But that is too much quick justice for him. And the government is wise. They have left *ChiMuti*, Little Tree, alone. He is free. He has his passport and he sits in parliament. This is a lovely punishment for him because he must see that we Africans can also rule ourselves and the Boers in a modern state."

Debbie was in the middle of a grin when suddenly, Johnny Macabe came barreling into the lounge and parked himself at their table. His face was red and sweaty, his breathing shallow.

Without as much as a hello to Debbie and Cephas, he blurted out, "Bill, I gotta talk to you," he scanned the table, "In private."

ivapo – disappear

"Take it easy man, you seem really upset," Bill said softly and kindly.

"You would be too if you had this load of shit dropped on you." Johnny was frantic.

Bill turned to Debbie and Cephas, "Hey guys why don't we get lunch here. They have ribs today. Let's meet in the restaurant in a half an hour?'

Cephas and Debbie read the situation immediately and drifted towards the restaurant to book a table.

Concerned, Bill turned to Johnny, "Hey Jay, what the fuck is goin' on? You look terrible. What's happening?"

Johnny breathed in and out and was finally able to control his breathing and his trembling hands. "Bill, it's a mess. I was collecting my pay cheque from the boss, Mr. Urozvi and he totally sideswiped me."

"What do you mean?"

Johnny gulped down his frenzy as he remembered in garish detail what had transpired in the headmaster's office. "I get to the office and the secretary tells me I have to see the boss. I thought it might be somethings about lab supplies and I innocently walk into a trap."

Bill was confused, "Jay, you're not making any sense. What exactly did your boss say to you?"

"Hah, it wasn't only my boss; there were two other guys there, big poohbahs in the village. You know how these Africans are, everybody wants to be chairman of this and chief of that."

Annoyed, Bill said, "No I don't know how things are at your school. What did these guys say to you to get you so upset?"

"Well, you won't believe this, but this Mr. Makumbe, he's a chairman of something or other, he accused me of practising witchcraft. Me!" He vigorously pointed at this chest. "Me of all people, I don't even believe in that crap!"

"John, that sounds serious."

"What do you mean serious! This so-called witchcraft is a farce. Oh yeah, you're from the bush yourself, Pickle Lake or wherever."

"Actually, it's Osnaburgh." Bill was subtly warning Johnny not to go too far, but Johnny didn't know about Osnaburgh Reserve. Fortunately for him, Bill had learned patience from his elders and he felt sorry to see that his biology buddy was becoming unglued. He tried another tack. "OK, John, what exactly did you do and why did your actions get the village chefs pissed off?"

"Well they said I was doing bad medicine with bones and then I remembered a week ago, I found a great full skeleton under a rock in a forested part of the village."

"Did you lift the rock," asked Bill, incredulously.

"Well, yeah. I saw a cairn of rocks and wondered if it was a cache or something. Then I took some smaller stones off the top and saw this skull inside."

Bill was shaken. His grandmother told him how the Ojibwa used to bury relatives in mounds. Over each grave the people erected a *jiibegamig* or a spirit-house. But the white man had stolen a lot of grave goods from his people so they didn't erect burial mounds anymore. He was incensed that this so called educated person was so ignorant of any culture outside of his downtown

Toronto milieu.

Bill rose from the table and said, "John, if you did that to my grandmother's grave, I would be totally pissed with you. Excuse, some people are expecting me for lunch." He left John stricken and alone at the table.

Macabe ordered a hamburger and fries to eat with his beer. Soon Kindo walked into the lounge and seeing Johnny sitting by himself, he came to sit down with his red-haired colleague.

Kindo ordered a beer and rice and stew and addressed Johnny, "Hey blas, why are you seated by yourself?"

Of all the Africans at the school, Johnny liked the ever comedic Kindo because he lightened the mood at any party and this gave John the chuckles. Kindo was ok and John needed some levity. "I had a rough week, just wanted to be by myself for a bit but I'm glad you came over." They chattered about the Africa Cup football finals.

After lunch, the restaurant closed for the afternoon and Debbie saw Kindo and Johnny. She joined them and they all moved out to the terrace to catch a cool breeze. Ten minutes of small talk ensued then Kindo went to help himself in the toilet.

When she was alone with Johnny, Debbie remembered that she was annoyed by the letter from the Club. She said, "Jay, yer a turkey."

"Now why are you mad at me?" He was exasperated.

"See this letter. I'm holding the bag because you didn't have the balls to stick up for your colleague."

"Come on, Debbie. Chafichu's just a trouble maker. They were both stubborn, okay." He had more to worry about than a meaningless letter from the Club.

"Johnny, why can't you make just one committed statement? Can't you see that one time the white man might be wrong?"

"Look here, Debbie. I came to this place to teach science and maybe that would help. Let's be honest. All of us came to see the sights and travel. We are not supposed to get involved in the politics."

"What is so political about what happened last week?" She was starting to lose it.

"Political! Come off it Debbie, Chafichu deserves to be kicked out because he doesn't shut his big mouth when he should."

"Listen Jay, this situation is way out of our league. These people, both white and black just finished a nasty war and there's a lot of unfinished business which we have no right to judge. And if they freak out on each other, we have nothing to say about it."

"So why did you put your foot into it?" He parried.

"Because Chafichu whose real name is Tawanda is my friend, in case you never bothered to find out. And Tom is a racist asshole who wanted to pick a fight by stepping on Tawanda's foot. If Mat Van der Merwe wasn't there, it could have turned into a real brawl with cops and everything."

"So according to you there's at least one good white guy, how white of you."

"Johnny, you can be mega stupid."

"That's totally unfair!"

"No, you're being unfair. You suck up in all the crap the Rhodies tell you about the Africans because you don't want to look around you."

"Let's put a stop to this. Kindo is coming back."

"Why should I?" She was raging quietly. "I'm not afraid to say what I think in front of Kindo."

Makumbe slid up to the table. "Come on, chaps. Take one of these." He handed them a cool pint apiece. "Chafichu and Matty Van de Merwe are inside. Let's join them"

Since John came to town in Debbie's car, he had no choice but to go back into the lounge with her and Kindo. As the three made room for themselves at the low table, Tawanda and Mat were deep in conversation.

The ex-combatant held the floor. "The trouble with you Europeans is that you have no faith in the system."

Matty was indignant. "Don't class me with others. I certainly do have faith in the system. Why do you think I called the cops three times on this thieving bastard? Now look here, Tawanda, you're a cattle man. Your people reckon wealth by your mombes. Now I can't help but git emotional when some bleeding skate like Chigudu butchers my carefully bred heifers.

"And the frigging cops are so useless. They say that they can't git transport. What rubbish! It seems they don't want to catch the bloke."

Chafichu carefully weighed his opponent's words. He nodded. "Murimi, the police are the same with we Africans. You can be murdered in front of their eyes and they would mess up the report. That is because of your Bantu system. Most of them don't even have a grade seven education. Yes, I do agree that the police are useless but please understand the reasons.

"Number Two, stock theft is very boring. Ah, why don't you bring this Chigudu gandanga to the *dare*, the Chief's court?"

"What good is that going to do? Isn't Chief Dhuma going to feel sorry for the poor black man and fix me, a rich white man?"

"There is nothing like that! If you go with that attitude, Chief Dhuma will not be happy. Like I said, nobody likes a cattle thief and I am very sorry for you. If you claim to be a fair man, you take your case to the *dare*, the traditional court. You tell the elders just what you told me and I'm sure Chigudu will be in serious shit."

Like all successful farmers, Matty was a born gambler. He took risks which were usually profitable. He accepted Chafichu's challenge.

"All right young man, I'll try the dare. How do I contact the Chief?"

"Come over to the school on Monday and I will act as a go between. You speak Shona. I trust that you will behave yourself."

"Don't worry, lad. I know when and where to move my mouth."

At this point, Johnny interjected. "Mat you're not going to allow yourself to be cheated by them?"

"What are you saying, boy? The Chief's court is all very legal in this country. There's less chance of chicanery at the dare than at a magistrate's court – no lawyers. I'm sure the bribe will be cheaper at any rate."

Chafichu looked hard at Johnny and remembered that he didn't leave the Club that night with the other teachers.

Chapter 8   Dare

"Now to tell you the truth, Uncle, this man is boring me." Mathias was speaking in masterful bottle store ChiKaranga. He angrily thrust his thumb at Cleopas Chigudu who sat on the pavement in front of the Chose Secondary Agricultural unit. At a sturdy wooden table sat Chief Dhuma and his two presiding officers: Mr. Chakurira – kraal head and Mr. Makumbe, no relation to Kindo but ZANU PF branch chairman.

Chigudu, the defendant, absently poked at a split toenail which peeked through the top end of his boot. Tattered, dusty blue overalls and a bushy black beard completed a somewhat disreputable appearance.

But Chigudu didn't really care what he looked like. *Murimi we Mombe was stupid enough to bring him to the Chief's court. The Chief was a black man, wasn't he? Murimi was just an idiotic mubunu for working so hard to keep his cows in excellent shape so that he, Chigudu, could make a killing at the rustling trade. Of course, it went without saying that Chief Dhuma would rule in his favor. He was black, wasn't he? That was socialism, wasn't it?* Thus, Chigudu meditated over his filthy toenail and waited for the inevitable outcome.

The afternoon sun threw hard but cool shadows where the other chairs were planted below the veranda. In one chair sat Tawanda who was upright alertly listening to the proceedings. Beside him Debbie periodically nudged him for a quick translation. Beside her Johnny sat with arms folded scanning the bird life in the mango trees behind the agricultural unit. Long discourses in Shona made him sleepy. And snoring on his seat would not make a good impression on any official even if he were a redundant functionary in the back of beyond bush -- so Johnny assumed.

Keeping order as the chief's police were two young chaps who belonged to the village Youth Brigade. They were smartly dressed in green ZANU party shirts and pressed khaki trousers.

Chief Dhuma interrupted Mathias to request, "Please explain why this man is troubling you."

"Well, Sir," Mat continued, "This is not the first time that Chigudu made off with my cows. In fact, this is the fourth time this year. The herders always find out who leads the animals out of the kraal or the pasture but this chap always seems to disappear into the bush.

"This time I thought I'd set a trap for old slippery fingers here. I told one of my lads to track him. Luke here," and he pointed to a slim youth in khaki shorts, "is an excellent tracker and he got on to Chigudu's trail right sharp. So where does Luke find the cow or what was left of it, but at Mother of Nyasha's butchery."

The Chief stroked his white beard. He was becoming quite interested in this case. Mai Nyasha sat in the witnesses' section resplendent from turban to toe in politically appropriate Zambia cloth. Comrade Mugabe smiled from both of her thighs.

"But Mr. Van der Merwe, why didn't you go to the police," the Chief asked.

"Actually, Chief, I found out from the police that this chap is a two-time veteran of Chikurubi Prison ..."

"That is a lie!" Chigudu bounced up from his perch.

"Be quiet and sit down, Mr. Chigudu!" Mr. Makumbe furiously motioned to the chief's police who

97

quickly replaced the accused into his former position.

"I am very sorry, Mr. Van der Merwe." Makumbe apologized. He turned to Chigudu and shot viciously, "And you. Have you no home training? You were not asked to speak. Your turn will come."

The bothersome interruption subsided. Chief Dhuma carried on his questions. "You are saying that this man stole from you four times this year and that he was in prison twice?"

Mathias was openly pleased with the way things were turning out. Tawanda was right. All cultures did have a sense of justice. And there was one thing that Africans hated besides sorcerers and witches and that was a stock thief. He smiled and resumed. "Yes Sir, since he seemed to be a hard case and seemed to laugh off his porridge holidays in jail, I thought I'd get more justice from your court. Perhaps he'd respect your judgement a lot more, being that he's from your area and all."

"Thank you, Farmer of Cattles. Do you have witnesses?"

"Yes, Chief Dhuma. Here is Mother of Nyasha.

She rose and a double image of Cde. Mugabe now beamed from her buttocks. Since benevolent cloth-bound potentates were the norm for women's formal dress, no one paid attention to the tapestry. Instead they nodded approvingly at her dignified carriage as she approached the Chief's table.

"Good afternoon, my Master." She curtsied respectfully.

"Good afternoon, Mother." Chief Dhuma

inclined his head slightly. *Being a woman of good character, she was respected by her neighbors because her bottler store was always peaceful. She even had two sons studying at the university. Murimi had chosen his first witness very well.* "What is your story? Has Chigudu ever come to see you?"

"Yes Sir, he has come many times selling his beasts to my butchery."

"Did you ever ask where he got the animals?"

"No Sir. I knew that he had inherited some cattles from his father. Therefore, I assumed that they were his."

Chief Dhuma was beginning to have some suspicions about this defendant.

Makumbe asked, "Did you ever wonder why he sold beasts so frequently?"

"I did." She said simply.

The ZANU PF chairman kept up the interrogation. "In what condition did these cattles reach your place? Did they ever have any marks on them?"

"Sorry Uncle. Mr. Chigudu always skinned the beasts before he brought them to me. He told me that he had another customer for the hides and he was doing me a favor."

"Is he a relative of yours?"

"Yes, His mother's brother is my father's brother -in-law."

The Chief took over the questioning. "Have you ever seen any of these hides?"

"No Master."

"Thank you, Mother. Mr. Chigudu, are you having any questions for this witness?"

Chigudu's eyes stabbed her in answer. Chief Dhuma was not impressed.

"Very well. Mr. Van der Merwe, you bring your next witness."

Luke unfolded himself and stood rather shakily before the old men.

"My son," Chief Dhuma began kindly, "Do not worry about anything. You tell the truth and this court will protect you. Why are you afraid?"

"Excuse me, my Master," Luke's voice trembled. "When I caught Mr. Chigudu skinning the beasts in the bush, he showed his knife to me and said he would bewitch me if I told anyone."

Suddenly the accused jumped after the poor boy and the chief's police prevented a scene by pressing the shafts of their spears against Chigudu's chest. By this time Chief Dhuma had lost his patience. His face blackened with anger because he was not used to such rude behavior in his court.

"Stop this one!" He thundered. "Your actions are revealing to me that these people may be telling the truth."

"But that monkey is lying!"

Then old man Chakurira went into action. "Quiet, you. How dare you interrupt your Chief! And you do not call another human being an animal in this place. That one is not allowed. These are very poor manners. Next time I will tell the soldiers to clap you. Sit down, you fool."

This time the court guards pushed Chigudu into his place and they stood over him. Everyone was stunned by this abnormal behavior.

Debbie whispered to Tawanda, "What a turkey."

"Ssh," he replied.

She turned to Johnny and whispered, "Iwe, you better not perform wonders ..."

Tawanda poked her in the ribs, "Sss, quiet, man."

Luke was telling his story, "Mr. Chigudu told me that if I told Baas, he would send lightning to my place."

Disgusted Chief Dhuma stared at the accused and queried, "Where are you from?"

"Zaka," spat the restrained Chigudu.

"Yes, I have heard that you *Dziva Hungwe* like to send such things." And to Luke he said, "Come, my young man, what did you do when he told you that?"

"I ran away because I got afraid. At first, I did not want to tell Baas. But my work mates convinced me because Chigudu was going around disturbing everyone."

"Then what did you do?"

"I went back to where he murdered the beast and followed the dried blood. Later I found the hide by a stream. I guess he got afraid and didn't bother to bury it." Then the boy pulled a stiff hide from a jute sack. The chief and his presiding officers examined it. On the left back flank were the initials HV.

"Mr. Van der Merwe," Mr. Chakurira called, "Do you know what these letters mean?"

"Ja, that's the brand I use for all my stock, HV for Happy Valley."

Chigudu's eyes were homicidal. Chief Dhuma faced him. "It pains me to allow you to say anything. But this is Zimbabwe and impartiality must be served. Explain your story."

Chigudu got up and jauntily walked to the table. He stood lazily with one hand resting on his left hip and looked directly at the Chief. The old man was at first flabbergasted at such effrontery, so he decided to stare down the young man.

The accused began. "All these people are lying. That one," and he pointed at Mathias, "is a racist. He hates me and is always chasing me from what he claims to be his land. Last time he even sent his dogs to kill me."

Chief Dhuma began to drum his fingers on the table. He was beginning to see why this man bored the Boer.

"And that woman, even though she is my relative, she is jealousy. She wants to cheat me of the price of my cattles. And that small boy, he wants to fix me because I caught him committing adultery with my young sister. Therefore, I chased him with my axe."

The chief snorted. "You, these are mere details. I have heard nothing about your case. Well, do you have an answer for these charges?"

"They are lying. They hate me."

"Is that all you have to say?"

"I am not finished." The accused arched his head back like a cobra and hissed, "I thought that when we defeated the Boers, I would be a free man, that I am able to earn my porridge. But that is not so. I am prevented by these bastards. And what is worse is that I willingly come to this court hoping for support. But I do not find any pity for a poor black man. Instead I find you dissidents believing a fat white pig, a retired whore and a brainless herd boy. I am now finished."

The accused crossed his arms and glared at the judiciary. Chief Dhuma leaned over the table and stabbed it with his index finger.

"Then you are very stupid. You have shown your contempt of this court and your attitude will be taken into account when we reach our judgement.

"Chigudu, Van der Merwe, you two go away with the soldiers while we decide."

Mat put on his green bush hat while he, Chigudu and the chief's soldiers, strolled off to the trees. The four of them sat in the shade and waited.

The three old men chatted quietly at the table. Within twenty minutes they reached their verdict. The chief murmured, "Very good."

Makumbe motioned Luke up to the front and the youth sped off to the orchard. Within seconds he came around the building with the defendant and the complainant. Mathias took off his hat and stood before the table with Chigudu.

Chief Dhuma spoke. "Mr. Van der Merwe, we are very sorry that you have been troubled in this manner. But we are happy that you have brought this case to us. Because you have done so, we can do something.

"You, Mr. Chigudu, you are a menace. You lie. You steal. You slander the names of your relatives and neighbors. And that is worse, you threaten to send lightning. That is very serious.

"I am going to fine you very heavily because this is not the first time that people have complained about you. And this is not the first time that I have warned you to mend your ways. First, you will pay Mr. Van der Merwe two cattles – alive please. Next you will pay the young man, Luke, one goat for threatening him. Also, you will pay this court one goat for wasting our time. You pay these fines within one month. If you want to be stubborn and refuse, I will send my soldiers to empty your kraal.

"Personally, I do not want such lying thieves as you in my area. You make too much noise for nothing. After you finish paying these fines, you will leave my area. Again, if you want to be stubborn and appear in this place again, I will send my soldiers to carry you over the borders of this land where the police will send you to Wawa Prison for threatening people.

"Do you understand?"

"Yes, my Master," a very subdued Chigudu mumbled.

"Very good. Now go away. Next case."

104

Johnny looked at Debbie. Tawanda looked at both of them. Earlier that week, the headmaster asked Tawanda Murovi, a qualified Shona teacher to translate for Johnny. Chafichu accepted this request because he was interested in finding out the truth of the gossip about Johnny digging up the chief's relative.

Tawanda gestured for Johnny to approach the table. Macabe got shakily from his chair. *He wondered why he was so nervous. He was no illiterate scum like Cleopas Chigudu who could be brow beaten into submission. No, he was John Aird Macabe, B.Sc. Toronto and no tattered old fogey with tobacco stained teeth was going to make him kowtow. Then again, under that checked jacket and dusty fedora sat a very discerning old man. The chief's mind was as clear as a stream. What amazed John the most was the caliber of his deliberations – if Tawanda's translation could be trusted that is.*

However, it was obvious that the old boy's decisions were both quick and thorough. There was absolutely no doubt in John's mind and that the Chief would not bat an eyelash if he had to send his thugs to cull the guy.

That made his case a little jittery. *How in all the screwed-up things that had happened in this place could he ever know that a loose boulder exposing d a great find in a full-sized skeleton could be this old man's great grandfather or something? That he educated, civilized John Macabe the scientist could be accused of grave robbing – witchcraft!*

Mr. Makumbe addressed the Chief. "Uncle, this second case is rather queer. As you know, for some reason this strange no-knees here – teacher at Chose Secondary – is in possession of the bones of your ancestor."

Chief Dhuma frowned. "Bring him here."

Tawanda prodded Johnny. They both approached the table. Chief Dhuma spoke and Tawanda translated.

"Is this person John Macabe?" The old man queried.

"I am," John said.

Tawanda whispered urgently, "John, call him Sir. And you must greet him. He's a chief, you know."

"Ah, Sir, good afternoon."

The chief nodded. Mr. Chakurira opened the proceedings. Tawanda translated.

"John Macabe, you are charged with robbing a grave and doing witchcraft with the bones of Chief Dhuma's ancestor. Can you explain yourself?"

"Yes Sir." John replied and it was translated. "I must say that I didn't know that the skeleton was an ancestor and I didn't realize that I was robbing any grave."

Chakurira held up his hand. "Are there any witnesses in this case?"

A farmer and a Chose Secondary student came forward. The farmer kept looking at John and shaking his head. The school girl looked at her shoes. She was caught between a leopard and a lion. *If she didn't tell the truth, the chief would get an n'anga to make sure that she did. If she didn't lie, her biology teacher could fail her and chase her from the school. Then the girl saw that the usually proud science master was also*

*afraid of the chief - shaking knees - so she decided to
tell what happened.*

"Mr. Guthusa," Makumbe was addressing the
villager. "Tell us what happened last week."

Guthusa cleared his throat and began his story.
"Good afternoon, Uncles. Last week I finished my dry
ploughing. Then I decided to go and hunt for some rock
rabbits in the hills. My wife makes very good groundnut
relish, so I went with my two dogs War and Death. I had
my bows and arrows. I saw a rabbit coming from the
sacred area where the Chief's ancestors are buried;
therefore, I didn't get into that place. Instead, I waited for
the animal to come to me. I sent War to scare the thing.
Then all at once, I saw this white man coming just from
the sacred area and he was holding a bag. And I thought
– hah, what is this? Then I followed him to the school.
He got into a classroom so I told this girl to go and
investigate."

"Is there anything more?"

"That is all I saw, Sir."

"All right, you can sit down." Makumbe then
turned to the girl. "So, little sister, tell us what
happened."

She swallowed audibly and began nervously.
"Good afternoon, my Uncles. It was just after study this
last week when I saw Mr. Guthusa coming through the
school gate. He sent for me because he is a friend of my

father. I went to him and he instructed me to get into the
lab where Mr. Macabe went and see what he is doing. I
got into that place and I saw my teacher taking human
bones out of a sack. He was putting them on the desk.
Then he mixed some chemicals and started scraping

107

some bones with a sharp knife. I thought he was doing some medicine with them. I got afraid and ran to tell Mr. Guthusa what happened. I am finished."

"Is that all you have to say, my girl? Why did you think your teacher was making medicine?"

"Excuse me, Sir; he took a certain white powder and a certain grey powder. He put in distilled water and mixed it. Then he took the bones that he scraped and put inside the chemicals."

"All right, thank you little sister. You can sit down."

Frowning, the Chief conferred with his colleagues. According to Tawanda's translation things looked pretty grim for Johnny.

"Mr. Macabe, come to the table." Chief Dhuma spoke in very clear English and Johnny was stunned. The old man saw his surprised look and smiled. "Well, you didn't think I spoke the white man's language, eh.

"You see, young man, I am the son of a chief. My father was a wise man and he sent me to primary school right here at Chose Mission. It is here that I learned English. I entered grade one at 12 years of age because I was herding my father's cattles. I reached to what was in those days standard seven. Then King George made war against Hitler so the government put me in the Rhodesian African Rifles. I went to Egypt to fight the Germans.

"After the war, I went to work under the railways. I retired from that place in 1972. When my father died, the people chose me to be their chief.

"Now tell me who you are and why you did this."

Johnny hesitated. He didn't know where to start because the chief's life history surprised him. *So, the old bugger could speak English. Rather devious to keep it to himself for so long. Didn't the guys at the Club say that Africans only told you what they wanted you to hear? They also weren't consistent with their judgements. One day stealing cattle was wrong and the next day it was ok.*

But John could not quite believe that because he felt that the decision in Chigudu's case was just. Another crack in the typical white Rhodesian argument was that, now that the blacks were ruling, they took every opportunity to pin down the white man. Why the hell did Mat Van der Merwe come to this traditional court anyway? Mat was getting a little weird lately.

The Chief's decision in favor of the white man deepened Johnny's confusion. Mat won the case not because he was a rich farmer but for the sole reason that Chigudu was wrong. And the way the Africans, even Tawanda smart ass Murovi, slavered over this dusty old man was another thing. Even Mat acted as if the Chief were the Duke of Edinburgh. Johnny thought.

His organization told him that Shona culture was as old as the Battle of Hastings, but the Rhodesians had convinced him otherwise. *What could he know? They were born here; surely, they should know. Johnny shied away from the obvious questions because it was far safer to bury doubt and uphold the belief in the superiority of his own kind. But what the hell was Mat doing here screwing up Johnny's view of the universe?*

Nevertheless, he was going to be diplomatic about this. "Ah, I'm a teacher from Canada. My government made arrangements with the Zimbabwean government to send us to come and help your people.

109

"I'm trained in the sciences, Biology and Chemistry. The O-level syllabus includes what is called anatomy, a study of the human body. We study the bone structure and make certain observations on it. I am interested in the age of skeletal remains for my personal study."

Dhuma thought that the lad sounded reasonable enough.

"What did you want to do with the bones?"

"I was doing a potassium argon test to see how old they were."

"Why?"

"I was curious."

"So, you find my ancestors curious? Young man, this is one of the ways that a cat meets its death." The Chief snapped.

"Uh no, Sir. Look I never realized that I wasn't allowed to look under rocks, Jesus ..."

"Listen boy, being allowed to do something is not the only point. The real problem is your ignorance. You should ask people where you can go and they will tell you. How long have you been here?"

"A year and a half."

"And you do not know how we bury our dead? There have been funerals of important people in my village and you didn't come to say sorry?"

"I didn't know that I was expected to come. You see the science syllabus is very long and I have a lot of work to do in the afternoons."

"Rubbish! You mean to tell me that if your neighbor died in your country, you would not go and say sorry because you had work to do?"

"No Sir. I know my neighbors at home. Besides it's our custom to send a sympathy card."

"It seems that you do not know us nor do you want to know. Is fifteen minutes of your time so precious? Listen, you, I am going to teach you a lesson.

"I and my forefathers are the owners of this land. We came here many generations ago with the kings of Dzimbabwe. The ancestors who are buried here send us rain. If they are disturbed by our bad actions, there is drought. Our cattles and our children die."

Unfortunately for him, Johnny began to chuckle at the idea that digging up a skeleton caused the gods to shut up the sky. "Excuse me, Chief, the present drought we're having is caused by the El Nino current in the South Pacific not by the gods of your people."

"You are a fool!" Chief Dhuma lost his composure. "We do not worship gods like savages. We worship the One God, *Mwari*."

"But Sir, please understand, these beliefs are not scientific. If you want to develop ..."

Chief Dhuma examined Johnny to check for signs of mental derangement. *This boy was mad or stupid or arrogant or all three. In any case the old man was beginning to worry that this hyena was teaching the children all kinds of nonsense.*

"Young man, I do not want to hear about South Pacific or scientific what what. I am very worried that you teach my children to forget their traditions. I do not mind about strangers who want to help the country. But I want these strangers to behave. I want you to learn how to behave. I do not care for your science if it destructs my forefathers' traditions. Our customs are very old, older than you. Thy make us what we are. They make us human beings.

"You, young boy, are very proud for nothing. You cannot go and say sorry when a *kraalhead* dies? You rob my ancestor's grave and call it science. Do you know that I can put you in prison for this?

"But Comrade Mugabe says that we must have the spirit of reconciliation. We should co-operate with our former enemies. I do not like this reconciliation if it ignores our ways. I will not give you to the police, Ancestors forgive me. I will fine you ten tins of rapoko for the beer and one beast to be killed for the forefathers and another beast for disturbing the peace of my village."

But that's over five hundred dollars! You can't do that! That's almost my whole pay cheque."

As Johnny protested, the chief became dangerously angry. Tawanda slunk into the background. This was too bad. He didn't want to be associated with such arrogant madness.

"That is not my look out. Pay at month end. Go away."

Debbie and Tawanda dragged Macabe toward his house. He raged all the way. "There's no way I'm gonna pay that old thief a cent. It's extortion fer a few bones fer Chrissakes!"

112

Tawanda squinted at him. "Jay, I am going to hit you. Keep quiet."

Then John turned to Debbie. "I suppose you agree with that old bastard."

"Yes, I do," she clipped. "You made a complete supremacist ass of yourself. I was ashamed..."

"I should have guessed you'd say that." He snarled and jumped into his car.

"Your Rhodie friends won't be able to get you out of this one!" She screamed after the retreating billows of dust.

"We'll see about that," he hollered out of the window.

Debbie panted with anger. Tawanda ungritted his teeth.

"Chafichu, how much time do you get for homicide in this country?"

"Debbie, leave it alone. You are fuming for nothing. He is lost."

Kraalhead – an area councilor

Chapter 9   Ndare

"*Gomeh, Gomeh*! Come to the beer drink at Mr. Munhu's *hozi*. Come and get drunk on the best rapoko beer brewed by a very old woman who is Mr. Munhu's grandmother. Bring your blankets because you won't be able to walk home – Gomeh eh eh." The strident call of the brewer's son filtered through the stagnant September air in the village. It was *Chisi*, the Sabbath. Tools lay idle in the compounds. A cat played with a comatose lizard and on the verge of the lane. A stray dog licked its genitals in the shade of a *mopane* tree, while a black chicken absently pecked at the ground. Tired men stretched their work-cramped limbs; exhausted women listlessly nursed babies; children lay on the grass and watched dung beetles push their spherical loads.

The Chief's court was finished for the week. In a slow confident way, everyone in Dhuma's village anticipated the news at the beer drink which was sponsored by the brewer under the mango trees near the big man's compound. The *ndare*, or as Dhuma's people called it *humwe*, didn't usually take place near a chief's house. This particular grove just happened to be the largest spot of shade in the whole village. Pairs and knots of people strolled toward the mango trees. Women carrying multi-coloured Zambia cloths walked three paces behind their men. A few school boys dressed in street clothes skulked around the outskirts of the grove hoping that no teacher decided to pitch up for a cool, tingling draft of rapoko beer

News was hot this afternoon. Chigudu the *gandanga* was finally being chased from the area. But most of the talk centred on a very queer case of one of the white teachers at the secondary school doing witchcraft with bones. At least that's what was collected from the local gossips that frequented the dare.

114

Tawanda Murovi was sharing as mug of beer with Mr. Makumbe, one of the presiding officers, while they discussed the case. Just then a schoolboy in blue jeans snuck a little too close to the knot of men. Sharp-eyed Murovi called out.

"Hey, comrade, come over to this place."

Foolishly the boy began to run away. A farmer in green coveralls stuck out his bare foot and the boy sprawled. Others dragged the fugitive to the smirking Chafichu.

"So, my young brother ... ah, who is this? Machingadzi, 4B. Are you mentally disturbed?"

Everybody laughed at Chafichu's mock rage and the boy smiled sheepishly.

"I do not get you, Sir."

"You Machingadzi, you are a monkey. You have only six weeks to read for your exams and you are playing at beer drinks? And you are on last warning before suspension. You are wasting your father's money."

"But please Sir, I am sent to give my relative a package of Madison's."

"So where is your relative?"

"Ah, I am not seeing him"

"Liar. I see that you smoke and drink and you will end up wearing a chain of U's. Go back to school before I decide to break your bones here. You will report to me at the headmaster's office after morning assembly."

The boy slunk off amidst general laughter. Makumbe giggled and asked, "Young man, don't you think he is going to run away?"

"No ways. He knows that I know he is a bloody crook. I'm wise to his spy tricks. If he absconds I am going to hunt him in the mountains and he knows it."

"Who is he?"

"Ah, get this. He is called Yasser Arafat Machingadzi."

"Come on."

"Ya, it is on his birth certificate."

"And he is the leader of all the terrorists at school, eh?" Makumbe surmised.

"Of course, but one time he was too clever. I caught him and another stubborn boy named Gabriel drawing breasts in their bibles. So, I took them to the deputy headmaster where they can discuss their case with the stick.

"I always tell my classes. My boys and girls, there are different languages spoken at this school. I speak stick language."

Makumbe doubled over in laughter and others began to drift over to hear another hilarious tale by Cde. Chafichu.

Somebody said. "Ya, that is very correct, Teacher. If they are stubborn beat them."

Chafichu continued. "Anyways, I gave Gabriel five good ones and Yasser Arafat looked like he pissed himself.

"Then I grabbed Yasser and bent him over. Then he starts shouting that I should not hit him.

He said, "Please Sir, you cannot beat me." They deputy asked why. The boy answered, "Excuse me, I am having tuberculosis."

Then I got hot and shouted. "Who told you that you were having TB?"

"No one. I read a book."

"Ah, what did you read," I asked.

"It said, if you cough and there is nothing, then you are having TB."

Then the Deputy got a bright idea. He said, "Young man, did you ever see a doctor?"

"No Sir." Yasser's whimper was almost convincing us.

The Deputy continued. "Hah, did you know that tuberculosis is a very dangerous disease? It is very very contagious and you can give it to all the boys in your dormitory."

"The colour began to leech from the boy's face. And the Deputy carried on with the attack. "Small brother did you know that we have to call a doctor to examine you? And then we have to call your father to come and remove you from the school?"

"Nn nn o Sir…"

"What is wrong now?"

"I do not have the disease anymore. You can beat me now."

Tawanda concluded. "Ah, a miracle of healing! I then performed ten minor miracles on him. He was very unfortunate that he saw me today."

When the mirth died down, another noise was heard through the now dusky grove. Two very slurred voices became distinct and the villagers heard a verbal boxing match in English.

"I really don't know what this is gonna prove," shouted a tenor voice.

A deeper older voice replied. "I'm goin' ta prove that yer a fucking idjot. An' I wanna git this story strite."

Makumbe gestured to Chafichu to go and investigate. But that became unnecessary because Mathias and John stumbled into the clearing. The bright platinum moon clearly showed their features even the red and blue checks on Jay's plaid shirt.

Being the eldest in the group, Makumbe sat up straight and addressed Mathias in Shona.

"Good evening Mr. Van der Merwe. It seems you are having a problem? You do not get here usually."

"That's very true, Uncle. I hope that I am not interrupting anything."

"No, no, not at all. You are very welcome. Sit down and drink some seven days with me."

"Thank you. I will." Mat signalled Johnny to follow him to a nearby rock. And the young man muttered something about a translation.

118

"Don't worry kid. The Chef's invited me to drink some beer. Very amiable, ain't it?"

Jay frowned.

"Ambuya Munhu's special brew." Makumbe first sipped and handed Mat half a mug. Now Farmer of Cattles, why is the white boy here?"

Mathias looked sideways at the now pouting Johnny. The Boer thought about the statement, agreed with it and began.

"You see, Uncle, I drank a few with the chaps at Mother of Nyasha's place after the court case. Then I had to see a chap about stock feed at the Club. I was minding my own business boozing at the Club on my way home. Nowadays my wife's giving me a problem about staying out late hours. You know how it is."

Makumbe really did not, but he nodded sympathetically. *These white men foolishly let their wives rule them. Too bad.*

Mat continued. "As I was drinking, this kid barges in shouting about getting cheated by Chief Dhuma. And I remembered that Kindo told me at the bottle store that John had been playing around with some grave bones.

"I just couldn't git any sense out of the boy because he was going on and on about this thing they call *mascientific* freedom. Finally, I managed to pry the story from him and I wanted to find out if it was true. That's why I'm here."

"That's all right, Uncle. The boy went digging around the burial ground. Of course, he was claiming that he didn't know. But he lifted the wrong rock and there

119

was Dhuma's great grandfather. It's a real shame. The young folks don't want to take care of their forefathers' graves anymore. What with the chief seated in the senate in Harare, these things get overlooked.

"The Chief was extremely bored, not by the young man's mistake, but by his proud attitude: that somehow because he was a science teacher, he had the right to do this and that our traditions are underdeveloped. The old man fined him heavily to teach him a lesson. Also, we have to pay a very big price to the *Zinatha* in town to send a very experienced spirit medium to rebury these remains.

"Since the bones belong to a royal spirit, this is turning out to be a very complicated business. However, one thing is clear, the boy has to pay up or we go to the district magistrate and send him from the area."

Like Chief Dhuma before him, Mat scrutinized Johnny for signs of mental instability. "Kid, Mr. Makumbe was just tellin' me that they're gonna have a devil of a time and expense to rebury those bones. Ye just can't use Dhuma's grandpa for biology class and that's that.

"What's worse in your case is that you got cheeky. You should know that the blacks don't go in for a big show of pride in young people. The whole upshot is, ya gotta pay the fine and ya gotta apologize."

Johnny was not at all happy with this rendition of the tale. He at least expected Mat of all people to see some sense instead of taking their mumbo jumbo for gospel truth. Johnny was not trained nor inclined to accept that environment and culture determine beliefs and guide emotions and actions.

And like most mediocre adherents to the scientific world view, Johnny's logic reduced existence to what he could see dismissing the subtler energies in the universe which the African never ignored and the *svikiro* readily contacted on behalf of the living. Johnny and others of his creed felt it was their duty as rational experts to wage combat against what they supposed to be the powers of sable ignorance and superstition.

Johnny dismissed history as inconsequential, and could not grasp the Afrikaner's experience. They came not from a mass civilization which ignored the power of the unseen but from the tail end of the Middle Ages when the remains of witches and heretics smouldered in the shade of windmills. Meanwhile the Protestant victims of Rome's pogroms fearfully huddled in their daub and wattle huts saying their stern Calvinistic prayers against the infidels. While Christians battled each other, heretics, psychics and worshippers of the Old Religion met in dark groves to drink henbane and seek visions.

To expect Mathias to support such a shallow stand as Johnny's, just because he was another white man, smacked of sheer presumption born of a pride in the material and dismissal of the spiritual. "And you agree with them too," Jay whined.

"Ja. Now you put yerself in their skins for a bit. To tell you the truth, if you were muckin' around my oopa's, grave, you'd be wearin' yer balls for a necklace.

Zinatha - Zimbabwean National Traditional Healers' Association which was legally recognized in 1980.

Svikiro – spirit medium

Listen to reason, son. There's sacred ground and there's free ground."

"That's if you believe in God. I don't."

Mat became exasperated with the boy's intransigence. "That doesn't mean a tinker's dam what you believe or don't want to believe. You do not own this land. It's Chief Dhuma's land and he has certain rights over it that you don't have. Yer a *maborn*, a city boy. I don't expect you to understand that.

"But you think yer fancy degree gives you the right to bulldoze over folk's traditions. This is the bush and here folk don't care how many letters you got behind or in front of yer name. They care about what you say and do. Ya just gotta pay the fine because the highest court in Zimbabwe will uphold African Customary Law."

"The Canadian High Commission can get me off." John persisted.

"Shit, do you have a contract here, or don't ya?"

"Yeah."

"Well then. You agreed to live here, so you must live under the laws of the land. If ya don't like it, then get out!" Mat thrust his right thumb backwards. His face hardened like a pre-attack bull. Corners of his mouth pulled down.

Imagine – Chafichu, Makumbe and assorted villagers, most with their mouths agape and mugs held in suspension. Strange things were happening nowadays.

Here a white stranger was scoffing at and refusing to respect the decisions of a chief – imagine. Then there's this Boer, born and raised as a racist, upholding African tradition!

Chafichu had never seen two whites arguing over the issues of race and culture. *He had always expected the expatriate to take the African side. But no, here was Mathias Van der Merwe, whose grandfather robbed the Majiras of their land, actually demanding that this puppy pay up and say sorry.*

Yes, amazing things were going on. Perhaps this Boer was trainable after all. Perhaps this Boer could change. He was trying hard to be fair. As Chafichu thought, deep inside historically taut sinews loosened and Chafichu found himself liking this pot-bellied, straight forward white man.

Then Murovi remembered the assembly point when a chap who operated in Gutu told him that Mrs. Van der Merwe fed any comrade who came to Happy Valley

Farm. Maybe the wife's attitude was rubbing off on the farmer. But where did she get her ideas from? As Murovi mused a big lion's paw clapped his shoulder and Mat breathed in a low tone.

"Can't seem to convince this boy of any sense. Let's drink. I'm frustrated."

Later at Mai Nyasha's the beer crate philosophers were hard at it. Topic: Science versus Tradition. Just to be difficult for the pleasure derived from being an ass, Kindo played the devil's advocate. He loomed larger in the candle's glow holding aloft his

brown bottle and swigging from it after he thought he had made a significant point. A local band, Devera

Ngwena, provided the background groove over the battery powered stereo.

"Comrades, study this situation in the clearest light." Kindo strutted back and forth in superb imitation of a lawyer before the jeering jury.

"A) Jay innocently picks a skeleton from the bush. Note the word innocent. B) He doesn't prepare poison to sort out his enemies. No, he does tests to find out certain things. What's wrong with tests?" –swig– "C) Since these bones belong to a royal spirit, some medicine can be made by a medium to bring rain." --swig-

He cradled the bottle in his arms. "Do you like A, B, C or all of the above?"

Kuda mumbled into his beer. "None of the above. All heretics should pay one crate fine. Come on heretic, pay up please."

"Ah, no." Kindo crouched into his Bruce Lee position. "I can do Kung Fu."

"Ya ya ya." Kuda lazed against the counter while Kindo parried with an unseen rival in the shadows. Kuda began to laugh. "Just like the time you wanted to perform Bruce Lee for that Rhodesian soldier during the war. It's a wonder you are still breathing."

Kindo panted, "Ah no, Kuda. My martial arts got us out of a very dangerful situation."

"And into digging latrine pits in an army camp for a week."

Chafichu and Matty were in convulsions over Kindo's antics. Chafichu caught his breath, "Kuda, when

124

did this happen? It sounds like a wondrous performance."

Kuda sipped and reminisced. The late-night crowd settled down on the crates and counter to listen.

"It was, ya, October 1978. All of us had gone to town to pick up supplies and we were coming back in the school truck. Of course, we were drinking. Of course, we had a crate with us. Therefore, drunken fools we were, we sang the latest liberation numbers that Chafichu's colleagues had taught us at a recent night meeting.

"That was very stupid. But never mind. When we got to *Ndanga* turn off, there was an army road block. This white youngster, about 19 or 20, shone a torch in the school driver's face and demanded to know why we were moving after dark. Poor old Mr. Mufambi, the driver, tried to explain about the truck getting repairs. But this kid pulls him out of the cab and started hitting him.

"We all kept quiet at the back because if anyone tried to protest, she or he would be killed for his trouble. We shut up. But the youngster wasn't satisfied by beating the driver, he told me to get down and he said.

'Hey Beard, ya know what this is?' And he shoved a bullet in my face.

'It's a bullet, baas.' We even had to call a little kid baas in those days. The soldier smirked.

'Ja, that's right, kaffir. And ya know wot I'm goin' ta do with it?'

'No Sir.'

'Ya know Grenade, don't ya?'

'I have heard of him, Sir.'

'Fancy that. Well this here bullet's for Grenade because he killed my brother. Got that, monkey?' The pig was shoving that bloody thing right up my nose. I could only reply.

'Yes, Sir.'

Actually, I think this kid was drunk. When he wanted to give me the kiss of death, he smelled of liquor. He cooled down a bit, but I guess he wanted to give us a nice farewell.

He screamed at all of us this time. 'All you fuckin' munts are heathens. I bet none o' you knows one of the Ten Commandments!'

Well Kindo being Kindo, goes into his Bruce Lee thing and says. 'Ya, I know one: Thou shalt not kill.'

You should have seen the look on the soldier's face. Oh Mother, he was on fire. He said 'You bloody bastards, git out!'

Then they shoved us into an army Puma and drove us down down Zaka. We turned towards *Makuvadza* Township in the middle of the night and the Puma stopped. We got out and would you believe those bloody Boers made us dig in the moonlight? Oh, sorry, Mathias, but they were very terrible guys."

Mat nodded. How else could he react? *Anyone living in Chisungo knew that the RBC told lies about the war in the bush and he had heard too many army chaps bragging in their brandy about culling kaffirs, not to know that this was true. And how did some really sweet kids that he knew turn into complete butchers when they were in the bush for six months?*

126

Then Kuda left the counter and stalked Kindo. He grabbed the skinny man by the collar and shook his fist. "Seven days and seven nights, Kindo, we dug those bloody trenches. See this scar on my leg?" And he hitched up his trousers. A jagged black gash pointed accusingly at the now cowering martial artist. "That's from Kindo accidentally stabbing me with his pick, the monkey: all because of four words. But it gets worse. Come the day when they decided to let us go, actually our headmaster complained to the army commander. On that day, the African soldiers were ready to drive us back to the school. Just as we were boarding the Puma, this same white kid comes over and says,

'Let the baboons walk.'

"So, we walked and walked and walked. It took us hours to find a homestead. But thank God, we finally did." Chitombo concluded with a long pull at his beer."

Chafichu cackled. "Hey Farmer of Cows, you are very quiet."

"Ja," Mat said thoughtfully.

Kuda grinned. "Don't worry, Mat, I didn't even notice your skin colour. I think it's because I don't have to translate like I do for those Canadians. But Debbie surprises me sometimes."

Mat sucked at his bottle still in thought.

Chafichu leered in English, "Hey, Murimi, come on. You are one of us."

"Am I?" More of a question than a denial.

"Sure, are you British?"

127

"Nya man, no ways!" Matty was getting stirred up.

"Well are you Dutch?"

"No, that was too long ago," Mat replied quietly.

"Then, who are you?" Chafichu pointed his index finger right at Mat's chest.

He looked straight into Murovi's face and said "I am an Afrikaner."

Chafichu whistled and did a little dance. "Brilliant, Murimi! Did you know that in English, Afrikaner means African?"

Matty also laughed, "You conniving bloody crook. You're correct of course."

Then Chafichu stuck out his hand, "Come on fellow African, shake me hand."

And the Boer took the ex-combatant's hand with a resounding slap and shook it firmly amidst the cheers of everyone in Mai Nyasha's place.

On the following Monday Headmaster Urozvi was shouting over the phone to the Education Office in town when Chief Dhuma and Mr. Makumbe walked into his office. Urozvi gave up his fruitless battle with static, stood and greeted the chief.

"Are you keeping well, my Uncle?" He clapped hands.

"I am well, my Descendent. How is the job?"

"The job is fine, Sir. Please sit down. How are

you Mr. Makumbe?"

"I am fine, Comrade."

"How can I help you, Chief?"

Makumbe spoke for Chief Dhuma as custom dictated. "Mr. Headmaster, I believe you know what transpired at the court concerning Mr. Macabe's case."

"Yes, Sir. I collected those facts last Thursday."

"Well, Headmaster, the Chief has thought about the consequences of having Mr. Macabe remain teaching and living on the school compound and they are not nice."

Urozvi immediately saw where the issue was leading and pictured himself writing a long report in quadruplicate to the Regional Office. The prospect was decidedly unpleasant.

"I am very sorry, Sir. But the Ministry has placed Mr. Macabe at this school and transfer at this time in the middle of the term would be difficult."

"Of course, Headmaster, we are grateful for the good relationship that the school currently enjoys with the community."

All through the exchange the chief browsed the cluttered small office with its neat files stacked in every conceivable open place. Periodically the old man glanced significantly at the tremulous headmaster.

"There is no question, Mr. Makumbe that these relations should not but continue as before."

"Yes, we would feel very much better if Mr.

Macabe at least did not live in Chief Dhuma's area."

"Would you accept it if Mr. Macabe drove from, say, a rental house at the mine and went home after work?"

Chief Dhuma and his aide huddled to consider the brilliant compromise. The headmaster wiped his flowing brow.

Then after a minute, "This is acceptable to the Chief. You will, of course, tell your decision to the young man. We want him out at the end of the month."

Once again, the chef wiped his face and neck. "Of course, Uncle, I will tell him after tea break."

Chief Dhuma rose and shook the headmaster's drenched palm. "Thank you for your co-operation, Mr. Headmaster. You are invited to the reinternment ceremony of my great grandfather."

"Thank you, Chief, I will be there."

Chapter 10   BEER MISTRESS

Chose Secondary School

P. Bag 8008

Chisungo Office, Zimbabwe
  Sept. 30, 1984

Dear Kenny,

Well, I'm still here rocking roots in Zimbabwe and still surviving. How is everything over the Pond and across the great prairie? The latest insanity to happen here at our little island of bedlam in a sea of desiccated fields is well – you remember the time we were in Nigeria and played the boozers' roulette with warmest Heineken in the deepest and driest junction town of *Zingeru*? Well this is almost as bad. In a weaker moment, I took on the assignment of Beer Mistress. Fancy title - rotten job.

It all started at an exceptionally orderly staff meeting here at Chose Sec. Sch. We were planning PARENT'S DAY: the day when Chose Secondary spreads its plumage hopefully impressing the fee payers – the parents. My H.O.D., who is an African replica of Che Guevara, became Food Master. He was to ensure that all the parents got fed this time. Our esteemed colleague was Beer Master last year and he took mastery of the situation all right. He and his cronies drank most of the beer! It was embarrassing to have the headmaster and an honourable Comrade Minister – two fervent lovers of the foam – sharing two pints of warmest Castle.

Now I love my beer as much as any aspiring alcoholic but I love Shepherd's Principle better: basically, the feast and famine credo. Shepherd's Law says: If it's there, pig out. If it ain't, forget it. As I write, an esteemed colleague of mine is drooling over his favourite fantasy: being locked in the Big Bottle Store in town with a four-thousand-dollar stereo system. Nowadays he's dating a very nice friend of mine, Felicity so Tawanda is on his best behaviour – some of the time. Since I was the only beer drinker on staff who didn't feel the need to bring take-aways to Monday morning assembly, I was voted Beer Mistress. Most of the women teachers were either supervising the cooking of vats of meat and rice, didn't drink anything stronger than minerals or were in charge of decorating the classrooms. I was chosen, unanimously. As I said before, fancy title, horrible job!

On that fateful morning, the chickens cackled in the fowl run across the path even before the birds woke up. My two cats dove into the mosquito net tearing more holes to play peek-a-boo with their doting but schizoid mummy. I should sell the little rat eaters to the Cold Storage Commission but they'd only give me fifty cents a pound which would not recoup my investment in those beasts. Besides I get periodically soppy over the lizard torturers. I usually set three dishes out for the felines: one for milk one for food and one for water. Kuda (My HOD) told me that his wife doesn't even use as many dishes for his supper!

Anyway, as the cats were pawing and purring all over the bed, I got up and threw on my one-meter fig leaf wrapper and groped my way to the kitchen and the kettle. BANG BANG BANG BANG! No, it wasn't an invasion from South Africa. A student was politely tapping at my door at SIX O'CLOCK IN THE MORNING. Now this whipper snapper was really pressing her luck; for on any other Saturday morning her queries would be answered with obscenities in the four languages I know accompanied by a not so well aimed club over the head followed by two malicious watch cats diving for the jugular vein and that is when I'm in a good mood!

But this Saturday in question was Parents' Day so I smiled sweetly making sure the kid could see the green slime dripping from my fangs. And like any other slightly deranged student, she would get the hint that this was not to be a regular habit if she valued her unmarked, chocolate brown throat.

Once a shower and coffee transformed me into a reasonably well scrubbed humanoid, Johnny came over and complained that Chafichu (Tawanda Murovi), Kuda Chitombo and Kindo (Tatenda Makumbe) were already half in the bag. They had continued their celebrations from the bottle store at Chafichu's house till six o'clock that morning. Since I am evil, I offered Johnny a scotch and he poured himself a double tot. They say tots for shots here. He finished it in five minutes.

Even at this hour, parents were arriving. Johnny rushed out to show them around the science labs and I ran out to make sure that the beer was safely and coolly concealed in the dining hall refrigerator.

What a scream, all the teachers with their B.A.s pitched up wearing their robes of knowledge (academic gowns). The Chef, Comrade Headmaster Solomon Urozvi (meaning brain in ChiShona) looked like a censorious pear in his U of London gold and scarlet hood and black robes while Chafichu looked like a t U of Zimbabwe pink plantain with an I'm Burning-Up T-shirt very visible under the black folds. I was resplendent in my Togolese Goddess of the Earth caftan. This motley crew proceeded into the church which also serves as the school hall for assemblies and special occasions.

By prior arrangement I stationed my student security force in the back row of the hall. They were trusty lads with extensive *majiba* experience of carrying guns and bombs for the comrades. I knew they would be similarly serious when carting the beer from the dining hall to the classrooms set aside for the festivities. When the Guest of Honour began his long speech, I snuck out of the ranks of staff and hurried the security team to the waiting school truck which was running under the expert control of the Mr. Mufambi, the school driver. Within fifteen minutes we had our precious load transferred without anyone except the headmaster being the wiser. The poor man would be able to get his fair share of beer this time, or so I hoped.

I managed to sneak back into my place when the Guest of Honour just finished his speech. After the choir singing and poetry reading, everybody filed out. Under the blossoming jacaranda trees in the courtyard the assembly witnessed the performance by the Drama Club and the Traditional Dancers: a troupe of very agile old men and their young female and male acolytes who called themselves *Ngogorombe*. For some reason the jacarandas have come out early this year,

These activities were scheduled for after lunch and I worried. Actually, everything went off without mishap until a semi-drunk teacher from God Knows Where Secondary decided to have a little fight with my favourite slug partner, the agriculture science master, very distressing. The village Youth Brigade finally cooled off the drunkard in a water trough. Not that there was much water anyway, but our guest got the hint. We never saw him again.

Well Kenny, as the cool Arctic wind is sweeping down through the Rockies presaging winter, here we nervously look to perhaps the fourth dry spring. August was very hot and one sultry afternoon there was even a convection shower in the township in Masvingo: the first water anyone within 100 klicks has seen since January and that didn't last long either. The other day I asked one of my students if her father was going to kill another beast for school fees. She told me that all of her father's cattle were dead. She said that this year the cattle died. If the rains don't come by next year, the people will begin to die.

This is probably the only country in Black Africa where the government is successfully feeding its people on its own without handouts. But it's water that people need. For the last two years at month end, all roads have led to Chose Secondary where the drought relief people are stationed at the agricultural unit. They hand out bags of maize, beans and groundnuts. Everybody from Dhuma, Shwauka, even as far away as the mine walk, ride bicycles, lag behind their empty scotch carts, tote wheel barrows and grain bags. From the upper vales, they come down our mountain with their toddlers running after like supplicants to a shrine. It is always a long, tiring but very happy climb to their alpine compounds with loaded sacks.

At the beginning of term the second staff meeting turned from the usual infighting and legalistic debates over nothing to the real possibility of sending the from ones and threes home, for we too must ration water. The once flowing water source on *Msassa* Mountain is now a trickle that takes two or three days to fill the water tanks. The kids are down to one bucket a day per person for everything that is drinking and washing. The water is on in our houses from 12 noon to two o'clock in the afternoon. We send students to fill every container to get us through the day. Chief Dhuma is doing a good job at keeping the spirits up in the village. People quietly and patiently stand in queues at the village borehole.

We went to the children and asked them what they felt about going home. Unanimously they opted to stay. The kids are willing make the two-kilometre trek to the silting Shwauka River to bathe. Though it was never said, we all knew that at least the students are going to be fed here. Even one meal a day in their home villages is not guaranteed. For the life of me, I can't conceive that the federal and provincial government would be able to feed 75% of our population for three years. A full three quarters of 8 and a half million people live in rural areas here.

Kenny, you're a journalist and you know there is a lot of yuk yuk about Africans and their inability to handle their own affairs and that we in the West have to feed them etc. and how we are superior in every way because we have money and all kinds of hi-tech gadgets. As my historian friend, Tawanda, says, "That's the lunatic ravings of a dying civilization." So too Rome foamed before its ignominious end.

The longer I am here, I realize that I am in the lap of a very ancient and tenacious civilization. Last year, when I first came, people brought their donkeys to eat the left over maize porridge from the dining hall. This year the villagers come themselves. There is no maddened scramble for the food as one would expect. No, the family sits down and the young girls take around a dish of clean water and everybody washes their hands. If they are church members, grace is said. Then the father serves himself as custom dictates and then everyone from old women to toddlers is served in turn. That, my friend, is human culture under pressure -- the highest expression of what we call civilization.

I'm very sorry, Kenny, I wanted to make you laugh with this letter but drought is not very funny. The old people keep looking up at the sky for some omen. The Zimbabwe National Traditional Healers' Association (Zinatha), a legal group of herbalists and spirit mediums went to the ancient site of the Zimbabwean empire to pray for rain. Everybody in every compound and bottle store says that if the *chimvuramabwe* come, then we will get rain. Chimvuramabwe? Rainstones – hail. Well, that's all I have to say for now. Tell me about your new newspaper job, eh. Till next time, keep cool.

Luv

Deb

Chapter 11   Rainstones

"My shoulder is paining me." Kindo rubbed a sore spot on his upper arm.

"Sorry, that is playing too much *maslug* for comfort." Chafichu dug his boot into some gravel on the road outside their houses.

"*Bodo*, it is going to rain and we are going to get it thick."

"No ways."

"Yes ways! Chafichu, you are a poor farmer. Look at the sky!"

Chafichu peered at nothing but painfully sharp azure set off by withered, dull, green trees.

"Can't you smell something, Tawanda?"

Chafichu was sniffing the sharp odours from the pigsty when Debbie came flapping down the road in her red tracksuit.

"You got a cold, Tawanda?"

"Nah, Kindo is trying to bewitch the sky into raining."

"*Iwe*, I'm serious. Didn't you read Geography? Humidity is high. Wind is coming from the north by northwest and my shoulder is killing me."

"So how is that geographical, madman," Chafichu sneered.

maslug – mini soccer   *bodo* – no

"Idiot, do I have to give you a lesson in meteorology? The blood circulation is affected by air pressure. When it changes, this increases blood pressure and therefore any pressure point in the body will feel the difference. That's why our elders can forecast the weather with their toes."

"Hmm, sounds more like Biology," Debbie muttered. She crossed her arms and quizzically studied Kindo for any other signs of mental illness. Meanwhile he took up his teaching stance jabbing his forefinger at his hostages.

"How manage, Einstein," she queried.

"You wait." Kindo checked his watch. "By lunch we will get something."

"We'll see," Debbie shook her head and then jogged down the road.

In his compound, Chief Dhuma sat waiting for his tea under the mango tree outside his bedroom. He rubbed his painful bunions. Then he too smelled the air. The earth seemed to smell fresher and the wind cooler as if after a long hot fever, where heaven tossed and turned in cloudless delirium, it lay exhausted after a three-year effort. Suddenly cool welcome drops of sweat appeared.

Two hours later grey clouds smeared the sky like lumpy millet porridge. Debbie lay perched on a perilous outcrop of *Zimunya* Mountain after her long run. For about a half an hour she had been herding clouds just for something to do. Now that all the dull-fleeced sheep seemed to be in the paddock, she was mildly apprehensive. *Hmm, time to start home. Does seem like Kindo is a walking barometer after all.*

139

On the back veranda of his house, Chafichu stretched between two chairs with his pant legs rolled up and his toes luxuriated in the cooler air. He turned the pages of a novel and the rustling paper crackled and scraped like a clumsy burglar opening a window latch. Even a blue bottle fly twitching his antennae stood still on a dead frog. *What is a frog doing this far from the dam, anyway?* The usually noisy weaver bird hung upside down in his papaya tree nest, waiting.

Chief Dhuma had put on a bulky green jersey for the temperature had dropped. *Ah, the spirit mediums' prayers were not useless. The Almighty is definitely going to give us something.*

After a thirsty session at planting, Matty got off his tractor. The black upholstered seat sunken from his weight showed a distinct patch of moisture matching the contours of his bottom. He gazed towards northern Gutu and saw a darkening of the horizon. *Perhaps too much to hope for.* He stuck a licked finger in the air. The thirsty sky sucked up the saliva like a toddler ravening at his mother's breast. Mathias had just driven the tractor into the barn when the dust began to swirl like three meter ghosts jumping into the trees.

All across Chisungo District the wind picked up the soil like a rug and shook out three seasons of dried despair and neatly laid back the earth in a different pattern for a good washing. Anvil-topped clouds bubbled out and spat hard white gobs and size of dollar coins which clattered on tin roofs and smattered on thatched ones. They pelted the ground dislodging puffs of dust before they melted into the womb of the frustrated earth. On the main road, a bus skidded across the centre line scattering these welcome white balls.

In his living room Matty sat spell bound by the snow like fall. He sighed, releasing tension from three dry years. *It's finally over.*

By that time, Debbie sheltered on Chafichu's veranda while Kindo capered and screamed madly in the deluge.

"I told you so. You wouldn't believe. Stubborns!" He cackled insanely. This infected the other two and as the rain stones got smaller and gave way to big liquid drops, all three laughed hysterically and happily.

Chief Dhuma serenely watched the storm gather its strength and blot out the landscape with a bright grey wall of drops. As the rain plopped incessantly into buckets, laundry dishes, and oil drums, the old man clapped his hands in thanksgiving.

Chapter 12   The Healing

Debbie lounged in an easy chair and slowly sipped sweet hot chocolate as a light rain tinkled on the tin roof. "Swan Lake" dripped softly from the speakers while one of the felines peacefully purred on her lap. The hot chocolate was meant to diffuse the several pints she had consumed at Kindo's harvest party.

The hesitant storms of October gave way to the first regular rainy season in three years. The exact amount of moisture falling at the proper time transformed the bush from its dry crackling cocoon into verdant flight. Within a few weeks withered greens and browns covered by a sickly ochre dust became emerald stalks of maize sallying down the terraced fields and draping the mud walled houses with a vibrant curtain. Mopane trees proudly displayed dark foliage, their straight boles glistening with thick sap. Bright red msassa trees competed with the rainbow of bougainvillaea gone wild: imperial purple, magenta, scarlet, burnt orange to soft white. Beside the mountain creeks banana stalks thrust up new shoots and pineapples sprouted new fruits. Down at the Chose Mission, the mauve jacaranda trees perfumed the air and the mangos bloomed.

Whether by foresight or by good luck, Kindo was the first, even before the day of the rainstones, to chuck off his necktie and shoes, roll up his trousers and cultivate the 0.5-acre plot behind his house. Soon all the other teachers and workers on the mission joined the community in coaxing the recumbent earth into production. Barefoot men straddled the rows and churned up clods with their long, heavy weeding hoes, while behind them the women, using short handled planting hoes, dropped a seed into each hole.

Very early each day when there was just enough light to see the difference between plant and weed, Kindo, Chafichu and Kudakwashe would be doing something in their respective plots. For they were the sons of peasants, whose education had neither sundered them from the earth nor from their deep instincts.

By the end of January, the maize cobs were fat and the tassels of sorghum, rapoko and millet were choked with grain. 1985 was a golden year. For the first time since the coming of the white man, the peasant sector produced fifty per cent of the grain. And for the first time a peasant farmer could sell his or her grain to the Grain Marketing Board – no middlemen. One woman in Chivi fainted when she received a cheque for two thousand dollars. She had produced one hundred bags of maize, a full metric ton, on her tiny plot.

In March, the GMB cheques were cashed. This signalled the old women to brew beer and all across the country families held ceremonies to thank the ancestors for convincing God to send ample rain. The Makumbe household was no exception. Debbie belched after a long pull at the chocolate and happily remembered Kindo dancing on the coffee table surrounded by cheers, whistles and cackles.

Suddenly the cat dug its claws into her thigh as running footsteps slapped on the wet porch. A raucous knocking rattled the front door. She opened up to Kindo and Chafichu now stone cold sober.

Gasping, Chafichu blurted out, "Debbie something terrible has happened."

She knew that when an African forgot to greet, danger was imminent. Kindo compulsively dragged on a wet butt.

He said shakily, "Some motherless witch has poisoned my son."

For two seconds Debbie was too stunned to speak. Then she recovered. "What can I do for you?"

Chafichu took control. "We need to see Mr. Dube. Can you drive us to the Club?"

"Are you sure that it's a traditional herb?"

"Positive," Kindo snapped.

"All right, let's go!" She grabbed the car keys on her way out the door.

Mrs. Makumbe waited at the open door of their house. She held her squirming son wrapped in a heavy blanket. Debbie reversed her Volkswagen Beetle right up to the porch. Mai Panashe got into the back seat with her husband.

The air became heavier as a new storm rolled in from the north. Thunder throttled the trees and lightning ripped apart the ragged clouds disclosing the evil which stalked the night. The baby wailed and convulsed in his mother's arm.

With her face grimly set, Debbie clutched the steering wheel and drove as fast as she dared. *Some idiot cow better not think about taking a promenade in the rain,* she thought morosely. It was a very long ten kilometres.

She finally pulled into the long gravel drive of the Club. Everybody rushed into the kitchen which was off to the side. Chafichu quickly greeted the cook, who was deep frying chips.

"Lazarus, please get Mr. Dube. It is urgent."

Within one minute Joshua Dube appeared trim and neat in his white shirt, black tie and dress trousers.

Chafichu acted as a negotiator for Kindo. "Good evening, Uncle."

"Good evening, my Descendent. How is the job?" Dube continued the preliminaries while he diagnosed the wriggling infant in the woman's arms.

"The job is all right, Uncle. Excuse us, Sir. My relative has a problem."

Though the situation was critical, this consultation was no mere visit to the dispensary for an antidote. The poison was only a physical manifestation of a deeper malice directed at the Makumbe family for its success. And Mr. Dube, as an n'anga was trained by elder healers to combat ailments on both a corporeal and an ethereal plane. Tact was required in petitioning the wisdom and power of the ancestors through the healer.

The baby resumed his screams and Kindo could no longer contain his anxiety. He blurted out, "Mr. Dube, I can pay whatever price you ask. Just name it!" He began to pull ten-dollar notes out of his pocket and Chafichu had to restrain him.

Dube raised his hand. "Please, Father, we want to help the child first. We talk about price later." He then turned his concerned black eyes on the mother. "What happened, Mother," he asked gently.

Mrs. Makumbe stuttered, swallowed and began in earnest. "Ah, Uncle, maybe one or more hours ago, Panashe started crying. I checked his diaper and he was dry. I put on more clothes and still he cried. I tried to feed him and he could hardly suck. I put him on my back and he kept on crying. Then he began to shake like a reed in a river. Then I told my husband and we both suspected something or someone."

The healer gingerly took the now whimpering child who was exhausted by his convulsions. "Lazarus, little brother, bring me some warm water and salt." He poured the liquid down the baby's throat. In a few moments Panashe began to vomit his supper. Floating in the bile were tiny green specks like a leaf that was crushed.

"Ccl, this is very poor. Whoever did this has prepared for a long time. Whoever did this, had to climb the mountain and get this herb from near the water source." The n'anga turned to Kindo. "Father, I must take this child to my home to give him some special medicine to fight this poison. Can we get transport?"

All this time Debbie was stuck to a spot in the floor. The whole situation seemed surreal except that Kindo's son nearly died just then.

She volunteered. "Will my VW make the road?"

"I am afraid not, Debbie. The rains made a lot of holes. But Mr. Van der Merwe is in the bar."

"Ah good," Chafichu breathed easier.

"We can probably arrange something with him," said Mr. Dube.

In two minutes, he returned to the cluttered kitchen with Mathias. The farmer quickly assessed the situation and solemnly greeted the people in the room. "I'm very sorry about this Mrs. Makumbe. What can I do?"

"We are needing transport to Mr. Dube's place and Debbie's small car cannot make it." Kindo answered.

"That's no problem, I can take you all since I have the canopy on the back. Right let's be quick about it then. You, Lazarus."

"Suh."

"Go and serve the bar. And if that idjot of a manager says anything, tell him that Joshua had an emergency at home.

"Right, Mother, baby and Joshua in the front with me and the rest of you lot, git in the back."

Chafichu clicked his heels and snapped a smart salute. Matty grinned, put on his hat and hurried the small crowd to his Ford truck.

Half way down the old mine road the rain let up enough for Mat to see the numerous potholes with his headlights.

Joshua and Mai Panashe sat still. The baby whimpered softly and periodically wretched more bile. His mother wiped him with toilet paper that Matty always carried in the glove box.

"Baas, I am sorry that we are finishing your toilet roll," she said forlornly.

"Don't be silly, woman. Use anything that'll help the poor kid. Mat glanced quickly at the two Africans who remained silent. He turned back to his driving.

Though the Boer was doing them a good service, Joshua Dube thought, *he did not know him well enough to discuss the more odious aspects of jealousy which often resulted in evil deeds. The less said about the sinister implications of this case, the better. The pressing task right now was to get the baby out of trouble. Then the witch hunt could begin.*

After ten more, bumpy, twisty kilometres, the rain abated enough to show a ravine. On the other side a neat compound consisting of four thatched huts, a two-bedroom European house, cattle kraal, and down the slope the ubiquitous Blair toilet could be seen. Mr. Dube directed Mat to the house and the people quickly rushed into its warmth.

In the sitting room Mrs. Dube reclined on the sofa and sipped sweet milky tea. Her knitting needles were retired for the night. When the door opened, she greeted her husband.

"How is it Dad? But it's early yet. What's wrong?"

"Ah Mother, the witches are active in Dhuma's village tonight. I must treat Mrs. Makumbe's son. Please arrange something for these other guests. The mother and child will come with me." The rest of the group, including Mat, shook Mrs. Dube's hand in greeting.

"Please take a seat, everyone. Father of Panashe, do not worry, my husband knows how to deal with these cases. Your son will be fine."

"Thank you, Mother." Kindo clapped his hands.

"There is nothing to thank me for. Excuse me for leaving you alone, but I must go and supervise the girl." She left.

Kindo flung himself on the sofa and buried his head in his arms. Chafichu sat at a discreet distance at the other end. Debbie occupied an easy chair and listlessly flipped through a newspaper. Matty sat in the other chair and stared at an interesting spot on the carpet.

Rain tapped out a soft rhythm on the roof and the coals in the *imbaura* cooled to ashes. The feared hyena now ravished Kindo's vitals.

How, he moaned inwardly, *could this happen? I have done nothing to no one. I reaped 30 bags. Kuda reaped 40 bags. I don't even have a car. So how can someone be jealous of me? Is this the reward for hard work? Someone wants to destroy my family. I thought I brewed beer nicely for the ancestors. How have I failed? How have I sinned?*

Kindo's stricken posture pierced Matty's heart. He got up and paced the floor. He hovered at the window and looked blindly into the blackest of nights. Mathias knew exactly how the young man felt. He remembered his own son Paul lying unconscious on the kitchen table while the doctor bent over him. That was twenty years ago and yet the same drama now unfolded. The same helpless, icy feeling assailed him. And as then, he now reached out to the only Power he trusted.

Father in heaven: if You really are the protector of the innocent, save this poor kid. He did nothin' to nobody. Does evil always have to win in this world? Why is it that Goodness hardly scores any points?

With that mute prayer, Mathias resumed his vigil.

imbaura – house heater, usually a perforated bucket with coals

The Tilley lamp hissed loudly and the Boer turned to see Chafichu grasping one of Kindo's hands and Debbie holding the other.

It's so easy for her, Mat thought. *The simple confidence to comfort a friend in need...* Mathias shared Kindo's anguish and in an outburst of feeling, Mat felt his pain. Compassion joined their spirits and the Boer began to understand that Makumbe was a father as he was a father – the differences melted away.

For the second time in his fifty-three years, Mat ignored the sniggering voice which threatened to block his actions.

Here jong, what's this? You're running a taxi service for kaffirs? Why can't they git one of their own people to run errands for them?

Matty heckled the voice. *You pick a lovely time to pitch up, old man. Whatever happened to your wonderful Christianity? You conveniently forget the Good Samaritan. Or is that only reserved for certain folk?*

Oopa threatened. *Mathias, the tone of yer voice is getting out of hand. You're goin' ta pay for this. Our people won't stand for it when they find out you bin keeping company at a witch doctor's place.*

Once again Mathias turned his back on the malignant old man. The Boer walked over to the sofa and timidly laid his hand on Kindo's shoulder. The young man felt the soft pressure. He reached up and grabbed the farmer's hand.

jong – boy (Afrikaans)

150

Mat said, "Steady on, young man. Mr. Dube's doin' the best he can and we're all praying for the little one."

"Thank you, *Sekuru*."

Chafichu squeezed his friend's hand. "Don't worry, blas, as de prophet say everything's gonna be all right. You just gotta have faith. Because when you come down to the barest of things, faith is all we ever have."

"He's absolutely right," Mat assented.

"Ya, chef," Kindo gushed, "Some people just don't want to wish us well. In fact, they even go to the trouble to try and ruin us. If that enemy wanted to hurt me so bad, why didn't he poison me instead of my little boy? There are some very cruel Africans, Sekuru."

Chafichu joined in. "Ya, that's right. There are some very wicked Africans who do this witchcraft. And I want you to understand, Murimi, that most of our people do not want this system. We are very afraid of witches. Sometimes during the war, the *povo* would tell we comrades who the witches were and we just killed them right there. No mercy for bastard witches. I tell you now: our people will never develop unless we refuse this witchcraft."

"What can we do," Matty asked.

"Well, if he wants, Kindo can make it a police case.

sekuru - uncle

According to the Suppression of Witchcraft Act, there is not supposed to be any accusation of witchcraft. But poison is poison," Chafichu replied.

Just then the door opened and Mr. Dube came in with a beaming Mai Panashe. Her son peacefully slept in her arms. Kindo was so overjoyed, he jumped up and his wife had to restrain him from waking up the baby.

"You see, Father of Panashe," she said, "Mr. Dube knows exactly what to do. I must give him only milk for three days and then he will be fine."

"I cannot thank you enough for what you have done for us, Uncle."

"That's all right, Mr. Makumbe. We will discuss about it in the morning. Just now all of you stay with us as the rain is too heavy."

"But Joshua, my wife will be terribly worried if I didn't come home."

"Now Murimi, don't worry. You cannot drive in this; it wouldn't be safe. I will make arrangements to use the clinic's telephone and you can ring her yourself."

Presently, Mrs. Dube and the house girl arrived carrying covered bowls and plates.

"Miss Goerzen and Mr. Van der Merwe do you take sadza?"

"I certainly do," Debbie said.

"That's wonderful, Madam." Mat's stomach growled in agreement. The guests feasted on maize porridge and chicken stew.

Two weeks later Mathias squirmed in his navy blue, three-piece suit as he steered the Ford truck down the highway toward town. Beside him Betty relaxed in her sky blue taffeta dress and white hat.

She had recently become apprehensive about her husband's erratic behaviour. For over thirty years he had been like the granite kopjes which surrounded their valley – straightforward, open, and reliable. Yet his old quirk of secretly singing Shona dance tunes in the fields made her smile and muse at the same time. It revealed that there was a far deeper personality beneath that gruff Boer exterior.

But in the last few months, Mat would sneak home with new LPs: Thomas Mapfumo, Oliver Mtukudzi, The Bundu Boys, Devera Ngwena and the Jairos Jiri Band – all the popular rhumba bands. For hours in the evenings Mathias would plug himself into the stereo with earphones and appear to analyse the lyrics. To get into their skins for a bit, as he was wont to say.

All this was perplexing but Matty's frequent late hours and mumbled evasions suggested that something more serious was going on. Then before last week's church service, two of her co-religionists: Cherub One and Cherub Two shared disturbing bits of information.

Cherub One, "Oh darling, have you heard the latest?"

Cherub Two, "Oh yis, something about Mat and Betty Van der Merwe, isn't it?"

Cherub One, "Ja, apparently our elder, *Mineer* Van der Merwe, has been playing around with a certain foreign lady teacher at one of those mission stations for those Africans."

"Oh, really?"

"And that's not all. Just last week I heard from a very reliable source that our God-fearing man didn't go home one night. He was keeping company with that lady at an African witch doctor's place."

Just as the two pillars of morality were about to launch into more invective, Betty strategically appeared.

"Oh hello, Betty," Cherub Number One enthused. How are you, darling?"

"Just super, Hilda, super."

Betty painfully winced on the memory. The blooming frangipani bushes that usually delighted her now inflicted their beauty on her wretchedness. She felt betrayed and violated by the man beside her. A burning anger left her immobile and cold. She was not the type to foment scenes. Instead her natural taciturnity built an impenetrable wall. She peered through one of the turrets and faced her husband.

"Mathias."

He winced because she used his full name only in anger. He sensed a row coming on. What a helluva time for a spat, on the way to church.

"Mathias." She repeated.

"Ja?" He replied tremulously, instinctively knowing what topic she was going to raise.

"It seems that you're the centre of the latest scandal," she boldly stabbed.

"Speak plainly, old girl. Just what or who am I supposed to be involved with?" He clenched the steering wheel.

She swallowed hard. "Just last week I heard Hilda and Co. gossiping about you and that Canadian teacher." The inner coldness iced her up.

Matty pounded the wheel in frustration. "Do you really believe that?"

"I just don't know anymore." She grated. "Why were you out all night two weeks ago?"

Softly he asked, "So that's why you didn't even let me touch you for the last fortnight? Luv, I told you the truth. Kindo's son was ill and I drove the lot to Joshua Dube's place. It was a hellish night and the Dubes insisted that I stay over. What would you have me do?"

She kept quiet.

He re-clenched the wheel. "Look Betty, I have never and will never sleep with Debbie Goerzen, or any other woman for that matter. She's just a kid for Christ's sake."

"That hasn't stopped you men. Soon as you turn fifty, you start chasing younger skirts."

Mat pumped the brakes and screeched to a stop on the shoulder of the road. He buried his head in his arms and wept.

Betty was stunned. She had never seen him so vulnerable, so much in need of her. A warm feeling began to melt crevasses into her polar edifice. The long abiding love and trust which she wanted to bury with her anger began to tunnel themselves to the surface.

"Don't you trust me anymore," he whispered.

It was very hard for Betty to look upon his moist

face and his stricken eyes. "You have never been furtive in over thirty years and this sneaking around is not like you and it has been so upsetting. But I love you too much to go on mistrusting you." she decided.

"Ah," he sighed. Then he smiled weakly. "You know where I slept that night, in a hut with Tawanda Murovi. The rude bugger snores." He began to laugh softly.

It sounded so much like the situation that Mat would get himself into not to be true. She had no other choice but to continue believing him if she wanted to keep her marriage alive. And that was the only existence she knew. Betty could not conceive a life without him.

She returned the smile and touched his hand. "Do you want me to drive the last bit?" She offered.

"Thanks, luv."

Soon their shiny Ford was parked alongside the Mercedes Benzes and Datsun Sunnys outside their elegant steepled church. A high-priced architect from South Africa was recruited to design the new building. He earned his hefty fee by sticking a fifteenth century bell tower on a Cape Dutch entrance. The nave was long and elaborately indented at each stained-glass window. African caretakers scrubbed the parquet floors, buffed the mahogany pews and dusted the oaken pulpit and white marble altar but they couldn't pray here.

Mathias led Betty to their usual place in the middle on the right-hand side. Heaven's white light shattered into an arrogant rainbow. Red tinged beams played upon the mahogany panelling and the cross shaped indentation behind the altar. Matty stared at the golden collection bowls, goblets and candelabra. He recalled the bare cement benches at Chose Mission and the faithful people who trudged across the burning veld to worship their adopted God. Betty scanned the program which was written in Afrikaans while Matty flipped through a hymnal.

The congregation rose to sing the first selection but Mathias did not join in. He stood apart, confused and terribly alone; for the Power of God, the confidence in his faith had fled from this place. On the precipice, his shaky beliefs and assumptions had finally given way and he fell headlong into nothing.

So, this was the punishment or reprieve for turning his back on his own kind and embracing the despised. He no longer partook in the Rhodesian litany of self-justification. Instead he kept conversation with black men. Was this his final doom to be flung away from everything he had ever known? Or was it a return to his beginnings?

The velocity of his fall increased and all the chaos of his soul was consumed by a dark fire. He felt painfully alone and afraid. Where would this end: in total dissolution blithering in a hospital ward or a bar room? Then the void which held both properties of darkness and light began to coalesce into form and matter.

His fall slowed and he landed softly in a green valley of light and laughter. And Betty was there to greet him. Relieved and overjoyed he thanked God ten times over. The pilgrim would be granted his woman: a source of love and stability to share his terrible journey.

No one greeted the Van der Merwes after the service. It had started already.

The telephone was ringing when they came in the front door. Betty rushed to it while Matty sped into the bedroom to strip off his Sabbath straight jacket and replace it with his T-shirt and shorts. Betty called from the living room.

"Mat, it's Rachel from Kadoma." He chatted to his daughter for a few minutes and sprinted out the door to his truck which had barely cooled down.

Mat felt restless and he needed a few beers to calm down. Fifteen minutes later the turn off to Dhuma's village swarmed with kids waving and calling out "Murimi!" Matty grinned and gave them a thumbs-up salute. Before he even saw the bottle store, he could hear the thump of the bass.

As he pulled into the dust parking lot, old man Makumbe called him over to the veranda. Matty had not taken three sips from a communal bucket of Chibuku before Kudakwashe stumbled over and grabbed his arm.

"Come on Murimi, let's drink" Chitombo was hysterically drunk which was unusual for him.

"But I am," Mat chuckled.

"Ah, never! You must help me drink my bumper harvest cheque."

Mat took a long sip at the liquid porridge, apologized to Mr. Makumbe and entered the store. Immediately Chafichu, who was only slightly saner than Kuda, hugged the Boer and dragged him over to the slug game.

Mini soccer, or *maslug*, was and still is the rage in the village bottle stores. In those days one ten cent piece or shilling was the passport to heavy duty competition. If you won. The champion reigned supreme as the challengers tapped the top of the game with their shillings, promising to destroy the incumbent.

Chafichu enticed Matty into a game. "Come on, Murimi, I have been waiting all day to destroy the forces of capitalism."

Matty winked, "My dear boy," he said in Shona, "youth is faster but age and experience endure in the end. Come on; put your shilling where your mouth is."

Murovi happily complied. He threw the first ball. It ricocheted off his middle line. He caught it with his front corner man and slid it into Matty's net.

"One for the forces of socialism!" The warrior cried. This game attracted a small crowd.

Undaunted, Mat smashed the second ball from his back and it thundered past Chafichu's keeper.

"What a ball!" A spectator shouted.

Matty laughed, "One for capitalism!"

While they played and screamed, a young town man wearing a pink shirt and designer jeans lounged at the counter and scowled at the players. He had totally misinterpreted Mat and Tawanda's good natured banter. This Mr. Jeans nudged Kuda.

"Hey Comrade, why is that fat, white pig here?"

Kuda turned his back on the town man. Chitombo bought a beer and gave it to Matty, who gratefully swigged on it.

159

Mr. Jeans was not mollified. He sauntered over the game and knocked Matty's arm.

"What do you want here, white man?"

Matty was annoyed and replied in Shona, "I do not talk to rude boys."

Astonished, Mr. Jeans then spat, "Ah, you, white man, you think you still rule us!"

Chafichu interjected. "Comrade, you keep quiet. You are disturbing our game."

The town man's lip curled up in derision. He stood a head taller than Murovi. "Who asked you, monkey?"

"And who are you, baboon? You are a stranger here or you would know the Farmer of Cattles.

At this point Kuda and three other villagers surrounded Mr. Jeans. Kudakwashe intoned dangerously. "Town Man, either you apologize to our friend or you leave."

Mai Nyasha's son, home from college and working the bar, retreated into the back room to get his mother. Mr. Jeans laughed incredulously. The joke was not shared.

"What is this? I come home from Harare to find a bunch of peasant farmers grovelling to a racist. Where is this: Rhodesia?"

Chafichu could suffer the fool no longer. "Fool, this is a multi-racial society and our friend has the right to drink his beer anywhere he likes. If you don't like it, go back to the Ghetto!"

160

At this point the town man made a near fatal error. He knocked off Chafichu's beret. A brown blur swished through the air and the maborn sprawled. In a daze, he wiped the blood from his nose. Half the crowd held off Murovi from finishing him off.

Mai Nyasha arrived and she collected the details from Kuda. She addressed Mr. Jeans. "You, get away from my store."

"Old woman, I have done nothing. This monkey hit me."

"Ah, no." She countered. "You started insulting Comrade Chafichu who operated here during the war. And you started shouting for nothing at Uncle Mathias who is a farmer here. You, we do not know. Go away before I call the police."

The town man was puzzled and angry at the wall of resistance. He retreated and shouted. "You are all fucking peasants!"

Kuda shouted after him. "We like being peasants, so piss off!"

Chitombo came onto the veranda to ensure that Mr. Jeans had made his exit. Matty scratched his head and sat on a bench. Chafichu joined him.

"Tawanda, what was wrong with that chap? I didn't do anything to him."

"Hmm, he saw your skin colour and went mad. Ah, now the shoe is on the other foot." He smiled.

"Ja," Matty mused. "Just what one of my people would do. But all of you chaps were on my side. Why?"

161

Chafichu shook his head as he would for a dull student. "Murimi, you're our friend. We don't hate the colour. We hate the attitude. That town man is a black Rhodie, a racist."

The Boer was deeply touched. Dhuma's people accepted him. He didn't need to prove anything. Mathias now understood that he had come back home.

Chapter 13   Too Long at the Fair

His red neck turned deep crimson at the edge of his starched white collar. Eddie Black, the Cold Storage Commission manager, squeezed his finger around this confining yoke and ended up loosening his tie in disgust. He looked enviously at Mat Van der Merwe who had the nerve to pitch up to the stock sale and fair in a more casual brown t-shirt and olive safari shorts. The still moist air from last night's shower steamed off the silken flanks of Matty's prize steers. "Ya got beautiful mombes, Mat."

Mathias couldn't hide his satisfaction. He wore a lop-sided grin. Just then a thick set African in a neatly pressed but faded suit, hat in hand, quietly approached the two whites. He waited patiently for Van der Merwe to finish sighing.

"Am I disturbing you, Baas?"

Matty turned, "Ah, Cephas. What do you want?"

"Are we finished with job, Baas?

"Ja, quite finished."

Cephas Madenga smiled nervously. "Excuse me, Baas; can we go to the township?

"You want me to pick you up, you mean."

"Yes suh."

"Where?"

"Tafara Beer Hall."

"All right, I'll git round in a bit." Mat then pulled the African aside. "Here Cephas, I think you and the chaps can do something useful with this."

"Mr. Madenga's eyes popped out at the two twenty dollar notes that Van der Merwe shoved into his hand.

"Ah, thank you very much, Uncle." He exclaimed in Shona.

"There is nothing to thank me for," Matty replied in kind. "You all earned it."

Mr. Madenga moved away silently with a surprised look. Eddie Black, also puzzled, asked Mathias. "What was that all about?"

"Ach, just a bit of a beer drink for the lads. They worked like troopers to git these steers in shape for the show."

""Well I think you'll appreciate this." And he handed Matty a thick brown envelope. "There's five hundred in bills and a cheque certified through Barclay's. Will that cause trouble at the Standard?"

"Nya, that's okay, it should be transferred within seven days. Eddie. Thanks for the cash though. It'll come in handy."

"See you at the sports club then?"

"Ja, maybe."

Driving down the highway later, Mat already had the ten thousand dollars half spent. He whistled happily through his teeth and a somnolent energy awoke in his veins. The brilliant sky dazzled verdant trees and growing grass with its ostentatious peacock blue. He didn't want to quench this spectacular feeling with boring brandies in the choking atmosphere of the Sports Club. He wanted to dance and sing.

The shuttered and sleeping town gave no promise and could never answer his sudden need to break out. The War and the Drought were over so why were his folk still nursing their self-pitying G and Ts beside stagnant swimming pools and burning tennis courts?

Now was the time to bust out of the laager and he knew exactly where things would be jumping. He wanted to grab onto the coat tails of the wind and fly! There is a necessity for effort and speed: like racing a stallion over the veld, stubbornly climbing the scree-strewn slopes of foggy Inyangani, and fighting the white water below the ceaseless wave of Moisi-oa-Tunya.

"Ja, them BaTongas were right the call the Zambezi falls, Moisi Oa Tunya, The Smoke That Thunders." He remembered how the lethal rapids banged and lunged at his rubber raft until it submitted to the unfettered, unthinking river which never stopped in all living memory. How was this uninhibited river connected to a dead old queen who was never amused? Or the fevered fanatic saint who renamed the mighty falls after her. Despite his wide travels and years in rustic villages, Livingstone never once set himself free to merge with the power of Africa.*

laager – a circle of wagons, metaphor for apartheid.

BaTongas – ethnic group living on the Zambezi River near Moisi Oa Tunya – a.k.a. Victoria Falls

Perhaps this came with being born here? Mathias did not know. He remembered the lukewarm beer he drank with Tawanda at Mai Nyasha's shop. In the middle of their eighth beer and after Kudakwashe's grim fable from the war, Tawanda had poked his chest. The young man's eyes were two pinholes of acetylene fire.

"Brilliant, Murimi. Did you know that in English Afrikaner means African? Come on fellow African, shake me hand."

Matty smiled broadly at the realization. He felt as if had downed three double brandies, yet he only had tea with his lunch. For about the fifth time in half a century he was totally happy: brooding about nothing and asking for nothing.

In no time his truck slowed down to take the speed bumps at the beginning of the African township. Tafara Beer Hall sat across the parking lot to his left. Buses smoked diesel fumes, kids raced in and around the ranks with their wheelbarrows screaming out their merchandise. The Dairy Board chaps cycled their freezers full of ice cream. Climbing in and out of the buses, women in a rainbow of Zambia cloths swayed under their burdens.

In front of the truck's bumper and right in the middle of the intersection a hefty woman with bulging biceps planted herself and hollered after her husband. "Father of Simba, come out! Or I am going to hit you again!"

Matty bellowed with laughter. God help the already beaten husband, who at this moment, was probably cowering behind a chibuku barrel in the pub. Reggae music roared out of the speakers in front of Tafara Beer Hall.

166

Bob Marley's tune "Is This Love?" was soon switched off and replaced by the local rhumba craze *Amai Navana Vavo*. And these songs of joy carried Mathias into the dark and smoky pub. Only one globe functioned as well as the coloured lights on a cleared space that was used as a dance floor. Four or five bodies were skanking up wonders under the disco lights and Matty recognized two of the jiving forms.

The Boer leaned against the bar and ordered three quarts and watched the pair of Choselites dancing on their haunches, snapping their fingers, lips stretched over their teeth, whistling wild harmonies to the tune. Under the lights, Kindo laughed as he fell on his rump.

"Hey, Chafichu, Murimi we Mombe is here!" He had to shout.

"Na, man, you are mad." Murovi kept dancing.

"And he's coming over here with two cold quarts for us!"

Chafichu did not relent between grunts. "Kindo – unh - you are - unh - hallucinating again."

By this time Kindo had stopped dancing. "Okay, think what you want. But turn around."

This time it was Murovi's turn to fall on his rear. Looming over him was the Boer laughing and handing down a sweating bottle. Murovi gave him the thumbs up salute as he got to his feet.

"Old man, it's nice to see you here."

"Ja, I thought I'd come and have a few cold ones. I made a lot of bucks today. Why don't you help me spend

167

them?" Mathias also had to shout over the music. Then the song ended.

"By the way, what was that music when I came in?"

"Aha," Chafichu was triumphant, "A new convert! It was reggae, chef. Bob Marley - Preacher of Rasta, Prophet of Jah. He played at *Rufaro* Stadium on the first Independence Day and the townships emptied; we were all there. He sang all the songs that we listened to on Chimurenga Radio."

"Oh ho, that's where you git all this Jah bless business. Who is Jah anyway?"

"Jah is one of the names of God. You know Jah is the African's God."

"Uh huh." Matty squinted at Murovi semi dangerously. "You really think there's a different God for you than for me, eh?"

"Isn't that what you Dutch have been forcing down our throats for the past 95 years?"

"Look here, son. You got this wrong. There is one God for everybody. And according to the way I was raised, some folk are more favoured in His sight than others. Take for instance the business with Ham the black faced son of Noah."

"Ya, let us take Ham for instance." Chafichu's face darkened as hot blood rushed to his cheeks.

Matty paternally patted his friend's shoulder.

168

The muscles hardened with rejection. "Now come on, matey. It says right there in the book of Genesis that Ham was cursed because he looked on his father's nakedness."

"And why was Noah showing himself to his family?"

"Well, I have to admit it." Matty sniggered. "Old Noah was piss drunk at the time."

"Exactly," Tawanda clipped. "Now who cursed Ham?"

Innocently, the Boer fell into the trap. "Noah, I guess."

"And you, Murimi, are going to base your whole racist theology on a drunkard's curse? Hah."

The Boer's eyes sparkled with wicked delight. "You bloody fucking lawyer." He intoned softly. "You wrecked all my arguments."

Chafichu grinned like a Cheshire cat. "Just so, Matty Dread. Now you're an intelligent man. Your people's belief that they are the chosen of God is born out of a medieval persecution complex."

"Hunh, where do you git this medieval rubbish?"

"You listen well, Comrade. You Boers came to Africa when everyone in Europe was still burning witches and Protestants. Granted, you were fleeing oppression but almost immediately you became the oppressors.

"God chose you when you were downtrodden. But since you began to crush others, He has turned his face away from you. Why do you think the Boers down in South Africa build their laager higher and tougher and deeper every day? They know in the bottom of their hearts that they are wrong: that they cannot disinherit fellow citizens."

"Just wait a bit." Mathias interrupted Tawanda's lecture. "If we're so cursed, then how come my folk are stinking rich? And for your information the whites built what is South Africa."

"Hey Matty, you better stop reading that propaganda *Today* magazine. And for your information, the devil controls the world and he is the one who hands out the pay cheques to the sinners. Check the New Testament, chappy. You will find that Jesus himself criticized the rich man whose reward is on earth. When he dies, he is going to be in deep shit.

"Point two: do you honestly think the white man built the skyscrapers and highways of Joburg? Black men cemented every brick in that city and they cannot even walk upon the same pavement after sundown. They can't even have a just share of their own labour. That's what I mean about disinheritance.

"When you whites went to war with Germany and Japan, you didn't occupy them for three hundred years. In a very short time, you left them their lands and their pride. You even gave them monies to build up their economies. But what have you done to we Africans?

"You think God supports the whites? Do you really think that any Boer sleeps in peace in South Africa? If black men are so inferior, why does the government have to build universities for us? If we are so stupid, then why have we mastered your language and your machines? Why are there black chemists and engineers?

170

And you Boers know so very little about our culture. That is our real treasure which you can never rob from us! But there are some black *matengesi* who are happy to give it away for dirty money."

Matty was numb with drink and uneasiness. This man knew how to reason too well, tearing down the last few bricks of his personal laager.

As was usual, when his wayward grandson threatened to decamp completely, Oopa barged into the farmer's thoughts. *Now jonge, yer really lowerin' yerself. You're scrapin' the gutter with this cheeky kaffir. Why didn't you go to the Club and drink with decent people instead of contracting foul diseases in this blerry pest hole!*

Matty couldn't drink away the voice this time though his head began to spin. *Hey Oopa*, he shouted across the neurons. *Can you refute this young man's arguments? Come on, Old Man, you think you're clever. Where's your artillery?*

I don't have to descend to the level of answering the devil's spawn. The ghost countered

That's not good enough for me anymore, Oopa.

Then yer headed straight to hell with this munt.

That's my problem, not yours, Old Man. Besides, I been outside the laager for a bit and I ain't dead yet. And I don't see no angel wings on you. I always wondered where you came from if not the Pit itself.

While this interior battle raged, the deejay switched on the perfect Marley tune "Survival" contributing a sound track to Matty's life long struggle.

171

Chafichu sipped his drink quietly as he watched his friend clench and unclench his fists. The Boer's face scowled and grimaced. He was fighting a desperate battle. The young man put down his bottle and said softly so as not to disturb but to call the attention of his drinking partner.

"You look as if you want to kill me."

Mathias was startled. "Oh no, lad, I don't want to do anything to you," he said wearily. "Have you ever wanted to kill somebody but it's impossible because he's already dead?"

"Ya sure, you must have an avenging spirit bothering you."

"How do you get rid of it?"

"You see an n'anga and he will tell you what to do to make the *ngozi* happy."

"I know what would make the bloody bastard happy but I'm not about to do that. Because he's asking me to think and do things that I now believe are evil."

"Ah, you are in trouble, my friend. It calls for a spirit medium to handle this one."

"Or God Himself."

"Ccl, you whites are very arrogant. How can a stupid human being be so impolite as to disturb the Creator of the Whole World?"

"Now that's a good Catholic boy talking here."

"Perhaps, but the *VaRoma* beliefs are very close to our traditional ones. You better get Jesus or somebody to act as a go between or else God will get bored and chuck you away."

"But don't you see God as loving?"

"Ya, when we deserve it." Tawanda quietly peered into the brown depths of the bottle in front of him.

"So how did you piss off the Lord?" Mat replied with a chuckle. Then he noticed Chafichu's abrupt solemnity.

"Killing my people as well as yours; that is the short answer. For an idea: I thought I was on the side of justice and I still believe I was. But the memories are not nice. War is very painful, Mathias. Some of the comrades did things that I thought only white men did."

"Like what?"

"Burning, beating, rape: I saw all these things. I forgot all of my home training because I was an angry boy, so I did nothing. I was helpless. Sometimes we became animals. . ." Chafichu began to weep and his suffering shocked, saddened and compelled Mathias to take his friend's hand.

"Son, rape and torture have always been weapons for as long as we fought wars." Mat kept holding Chafichu's hand like he had done with all of his children when they were distressed. "The English did exactly the same things to my people." With a pang of disgust Mathias recalled *white Rhodesian army chaps bragging in their brandy about shagging black pig and culling kaffirs. And he now understood why an otherwise intelligent, funny and generous person like Tawanda Murovi could be such a stubborn, argumentative fool at times. He was in pain.*

"This I know, shamwari," Tawanda wiped his eyes and replied, "I will always support justice for everyone, but not with the gun. War made us, made me worse than the wildest hyena. It almost destructed my humanity. And what is my penance?

"Many nights the ghosts of the Rhodesians and black sell-outs visit me. I cannot forget their eyes. Some scorn me and others pleaded for their lives like they did before. I have much to answer for when I meet my ancestors."

"You have to try and forget this. Let's drink," Matty advised.

"Better idea," Chafich agreed.

Chapter 14   Picked Up

Constable Chigwede was on the lookout for drunkards. With the annual stock sale and cattle fair in full swing, there were thousands of thirsty farmers, business owners, public service workers, and chefs converging on the town. Resourceful thieves also came to reap a rich harvest of bulging wallets.

Chigwede, an evangelistic Fanta drinker and thereby the laughing stock of his less abstemious colleagues, hated all of them and was going to fix each one of these undisciplined monkeys. Subduing drunkards lent this unctuous little man a solemn omnipotence which, without his uniform and badge, Chigwede would never have wielded over his fellows. These and other reasons compelled the section officer to post him opposite the Afrikaner church on the eastern road leading out of town.

He first heard the slurred and boisterous singing. "*Nhamo, nhamo, nhamo.*" Rubbing his hands in anticipation he waved the Ford pick-up to stop at the barrier. The truck knocked over the barrier and the constable went angrily to the back of the truck where farm workers lolled in their now wrinkled Sunday best. Half - filled chibuku cartons and quart bottles vanished under legs and benches.

Chigwede strode to the cab. "You, get down." His rough Shona sentence was cut off by shock. Leering out the window was an extremely drunk, tomato- faced Boer with a quart bottle balanced between his bare knees.

"*Manheru Mineer*, hic." Mathias tried to focus on the policeman.

Manheru – Good evening.

"Your license." Chigwede snapped in English.

Mathias belched as he reached for his wallet. He swung his hand too far knocking the quart and dropping the wallet under a steady stream of Black Label.

"Excuse me, Uncle." Mat smiled weakly.

"Idiot, you are dead drunk and I don't need your bad Shona."

The person that Chigwede hated more than a disorderly drunk was a friendly white drunkard who treated him as a non-entity when sober. The license was in order but this fool would kill himself and ten other people before he went twenty more kilometres.

"Iwe, you are too drunk. Your passengers want to go home not to their graves." He snatched the keys out of the ignition and Mathias blew a blood vessel.

"You tin-plated little munt, gimme my keys!"

Chigwede smiled venomously. "So from mineer to munt. You are very stupid. I am going to arrest you. Get out!"

Seeing the black complexion of the policeman tighten, Mat calmed down. *This is a real mean bugger. Gotta be careful,* he thought. Then he had trouble finding the door handle and ended up closing the window. Impatiently Chigwede yanked the door open and just caught the Boer as he fell out of the truck.

The passengers glumly alighted and headed for the bus rank. Chigwede led the lurching Boer down the street. When they skirted the roundabout, he visibly quailed at the sight of the Synod building. Two office lights were on. Mathias knew Reverend Van Rooi was

176

preparing for the general board meeting in the morning. And to his utter desolation, Mathias recalled that he was a board member and that his presence was required.

"Please, ossifer, you can march right down the main street but not here," he pleaded.

Chigwede noted the Synod building with sadistic satisfaction. He quietly jeered. "Boer, you are going where I tell you to go. Keep moving."

Mathias stumbled on the slope outside the bakery. "Hey drunkard, you want me to put the handcuffs on you?"

Reverend Van Rooi, Secretary General of the Synod, got up from his work, stretched and looked out the window. He was a spare man, balding with brown freckles on his face and arms. He loved to rest his eyes on the bougainvillea bushes blooming along the avenue. Then he saw the policeman leading a tipsy white farmer. His t- shirt stuck to his back, khaki shorts hung down to his thighs and feet scuffed along the pavement.

"Reverend, come here." He summoned his colleague. Reverend Mapfumo.

"Yes Mr. Van Rooi, what is wrong?"

"Look at this spectacle." His face became granite hard.

"*Mai we*, is that *Oom* Mathias?"

Mai we – Oh mother.   *Oom (Afrikaans)* – uncle

177

"Ja, he's stinking drunk."

"Ccl, this is very poor." The African clicked in disgust. "Surely God meant for us to see this!" Mapfumo always waxed apocalyptic when shocked.

"Evidently so, Reverend. We must do something about this." Van Rooi's voice grated like an axe being sharpened on a stone. "I will talk to him after the meeting tomorrow."

"Very wise, Reverend, very wise." Mapfumo murmured in agreement.

Chapter 15   Matty's Dread

Veld fire! Yellow death licked the grass and the despairing blades curled ashen. Choking, burning smoke led the assault on all that lived and Mathias ran. Keening and wailing rose above the furious conflagration. On the deathward side of the flame wall, thousands upon thousands of white stricken faces wrenched from astonishment, to surprise, then horror, finally to self-pity. Still he ran and the boiler hot wind melted the t-shirt to his back. And a voice, different from that of the malevolent grandfather, a tough but fair voice, roared inside his brain. "Viper: who warned you to flee the wrath to come?"

Rocks speared through the molten leather of his boots -- but he had no boots. His socks were shredded ankle laces. Mat began to stumble on the gravel of the plain; his bleeding feet could no longer hold him up. A searing lump circled his chest in ominous warning like a welding torch piercing metal. "Stop running!" His neurons commanded. But the flames gulped at the earth just behind him.

Is this the way his world would end? Not with a fused blast but an aging man's simper? Falling, scraping elbows and knees, he thought *it would be half pleasant just to lie here and get roasted: braaied boerewors marinated in beer*. His laugh was a raspy cackle. Then he saw them.

Through sweat bleared eyes, Mathias blinked on a river with fresh green baobab trees. Baobabs growing by a river, strange? Palms and olives accompanied the bulbous monstrosities that God had turned upside down.

braai (Afrikaans) - barbecue

179

Thick rain forest undergrowth skirted the trees and gradually gave way to a grassy sward that stretched right to the water's edge. Dozens of people came singly down to the bank.

Mathias watched fascinated as a small-boned yellow woman guided a big black man into the water. She dunked him and he submitted. Then she left and the black remained. Then a white man came into the river and the process was repeated. The white stayed behind to baptize a brown woman. It continued. There seemed to be no official at this ceremony. Supplicants became priests became congregants. The grass was littered with small groups of congregants of both genders and all shades. Clearly there were hundreds of people here but the forest and grassy beach lent each group ample room.

One communicant soon to be a priest motioned to Mathias from the middle of the river. The Boer wiped all the sweat from his eyes and his mouth flew open in joyful shock. Then his lip curled up in mock derision.

"Chafichu, you troublesome jackal, what are you doing here?" Mat laughed happily, forgetting about the ash in his throat. He limped across to the bank on the flame side

"Come on in, Mat. The water is very nice."

As soon as his seared and bleeding flesh touched the cool water, Mat winced. But the lower temperature felt good. Despite the pain, he felt strength returning to his tortured feet. The welder's torch no longer burned in his chest.

"Chafichu," he asked, relieved that at least knew someone here, "what is this place?"

"Well," Tawanda scratched his beard and thought, "A) a refuge, B) the past, C) the future, or D) all of the above." He giggled.

"Cheeky, Tawanda, too cheeky. So what are you doin' here? Ja, I forgot. You're a History teacher. You probably made all this up."

"Do not blaspheme, Matty Dread. I am only a mote in God's eye. But to answer your question, chef, sometimes half-mad comrades get a chance to repent."

"For what?"

"Killing my people as well as yours; that is the short answer. But the memories are not nice. War is very painful, Mathias. Some of the comrades did things that I thought only white men did."

"Like what?"

"Burning, beating, rape: I saw all these things. I forgot all my home training because I was an angry boy, so I did nothing."

"Son, rape and torture have always been weapons for as long as we have wars. The English did exactly the same things to my people."

"This I know, shamwari," Tawanda replied, "I will always support justice for everyone, but not with the gun. War made us, made me worse than the wildest hyena, it almost destructed my humanity. Now what is my penance? I cannot forget the eyes of the Rhodesians and black sell-outs. Some scorned me and others pleaded for their lives. I have much to answer for. Therefore, I need to be here as much as you do."

"I still don't get this," Mathias was still confused by the ceremony.

"This is a place of healing. But you better get wet first like I did."

"Is this really necessary?" In answer, Chafichu stretched his hand backward to where the flames had completely decimated the people behind. Nothing but heaps of ashes was left on the floor of the desert.

"Do you want to go back there, my friend? You have no other choice."

"I guess not," Matty sighed.

"Come on, blas, don't be so glum. It is really quite nice. Clears away the babalazi."

Mathias chuckled and relented. The mucky brown depths acted as mirror and he was able to see everything about himself. This revelation was very uncomfortable. Not only his actions but even his existence was questioned and criticized. Again, that rough compassionate voice now rose in a cadence of infinite power and love.

"You will now go before the rulers of your people. Your name will be slandered and you will be accused of false things. But do not despair in answering such charges; for I will give you words with which to speak. You will be cast out from their assemblies as a traitor but do not fear; for I am with you."

Something heavy, but movable, blocked Matty's ascent to the surface. He flailed his arms and found himself awake with a punishing headache. Sore back, restless sleep, small cot with a lumpy mattress; he was in a cell in the town jail. Presently, a brown face peered through the bars. That face was about to leer, but Matty's grey complexion stopped the guard's routine torment of hungover prisoners.

"Old man: what is wrong with you?"

Mathias stood up, stretched, and rubbed his chest. No pain He frowned. "I'm all right, thanks. Could I have a glass of water?"

Relieved that this white man wasn't going to have a heart attack on his shift, the guard sneered, "So, chef, you want some water? There are no tumblers here." He was just turning to leave.

"Please," Matt y lurched to the bars and stuck his nose through. What time is it? Can I get out of here? I don't care if I have to drink from a bleeding bucket."

"Slow down, old man. Do you know your name now?"

"Of course, Mathias Paul Van der Merwe." Then he winced because he sounded either like a lobotomized moron or an extremely dull school boy.

"Better. You didn't know it last night."

"Hunh?"

"You were over drunk."

Matty sighed, "Ja, I guess so." His head sunk into his crossed arms.

The guard shook his own head. "You know, old man., we Africans do not like to see you Europeans suffering." He smiled sardonically.

I bet you don't. Matty silently fumed.

"Be patient and I will check with the desk sergeant about you."

Mathias could only sit and wait. Still this gave him time to figure out that weird dream of his. Usually he didn't remember them too often, but that voice he could never forget. Soon this reverie was crudely interrupted by a falsetto petition.

"Hey, Daddy, give me fire." The source of the wheedling came from a tousled African.

Matty held his painful head and feared that he might be over the edge. He cocked an eye on his cell mate. "What d'ya say?"

"You gotta match old man?" His cell mate dangled a roughly rolled cigarette from the left side of his mouth.

"Hey, is that legal smoke or dagga? Besides, I ain't got no matches."

"What if it is not legal? What can you do about it anyways?"

Mathias looked between the bars as an orderly came down the aisle pushing a cart loaded with steaming pots and stacked bowls.

"Breakfast, Comrades. You better eat before it's gone."

Two enamel bowls were shoved under the grate of their cell. Mat took one taste and discovered that there was no sugar to make the bland maize porridge more

184

edible. He ate three tablespoons and shoved the bowl under his cot. His cellmate grinned at him.

"Not hungry, chef? This is not the Harare Sheraton, you know."

"You're not bloody joking. The whole world seems to know that I got soused last night. What are you in for?"

"State secret." His cell mate smiled showing tobacco - stained teeth.

Mathias lay back on his cot and closed his eyes. *No one,* he thought, *had better know where I spent the night. Bad enough the truck's been impounded for God knows how long.* That he had landed in the town drunk tank was too disgraceful to even contemplate. He shoved the brooding implications into the background and concentrated on the task of trying to find out what time it was as there was no window in the cell.

The coppers had taken his watch along with his wallet, boots and hat; standard procedure for hysterical drunkards. The orderly came back along the cells collecting the bowls and behind him came the guard.

"Mathias Van der Merwe. Oh, that's you, old man."

He rushed to the bars. "Yis?"

"The desk sergeant wants to see you."

Matty closed his eyes in relief. *Thank God.*

A balding powerful man sat at the counter, his well- developed biceps tried to burst through the brown uniform.

"Mathias Paul Vander Merwe. So, chef, did you enjoy your rest?"

Matty scowled. He said nothing.

"You made a lot of noise for nothing last night."

"What are my charges, sergeant?"

"Public intoxication, disturbing the peace and drunk driving."

Mat frowned, "So what will happen to me?"

"Well, the first two charges are nothing. Each carries a twenty-dollar fine but you will go to court for the third charge. Are you having forty dollars?"

"I better have."

"Sign these forms." The officer shoved two official documents toward the farmer. "One is for admission of guilt and the other is to verify that we are having your truck." He then took a fat, large manila envelope from under the Formica counter and poured out the contents. "Make sure you are having everything. I do not want you returning back shouting that we took something."

Mat checked his belongings and nodded. He got the receipts for the paid fines and started to slouch out the door. The sergeant gleefully called after him.

"Hey, Sekuru, you are forgetting your boots."

The Boer felt a nervous tingling in the pit of his stomach as his testicles ascended into his abdomen. All his instincts urged him to miss this meeting and crawl off home to bed. But something forced him to walk through the door and quietly slip into the boardroom. He sat against the wall hoping to be inconspicuous. But the frantic sponge bath in the hotel washroom had not quite masked the odour of Tafara Beer Hall. He smelt like a goat and felt like a monkey. Mat's entrance did not go unnoticed by this assembly of elders. Reverend Van Rooi was chairing the meeting. His lackey, Rev. Mapfumo, hurriedly took notes.

Rev. Van Rooi rubbed his eyes, looked at Van der Merwe and announced the next item on the agenda. "Now to discipline." Smiling, he turned to the farmer. "Good morning, Mr. Van der Merwe. I'm glad that you could finally make it." But his curved lips did not diminish the glacial stare. "In fact, Mineer, you have the dubious honour of being mentioned on our agenda."

"Oh." Mathias sank back in his chair prepared for the worst.

"According to a report from our church members," and here the cleric raised his eyebrows significantly at the Boer, "Mr. Van der Merwe you have not acted in a way befitting an elder of this church."

"Speak clearly, Reverend. What exactly is behaviour befitting an elder?" Despite his bold and quick retort, his stomach muscles tightened.

"You tell us, Mineer. You have been frequenting beer halls where prostitutes are known to conduct their business. You have been seen at these shebeens both in town and in the rural areas. Your prodigious drinking bouts with Africans have acquired you some notoriety in

the province. Just by looking at you now, it seems that you didn't prepare well for this meeting. Your inappropriate manner of dress looks slept in.

187

"But the more serious charge is that you have been having an affair with an expatriate teacher. How do you answer to that?"

Mathias flew to his feet, his hangover forgotten in what became that singular moment when he had to defend his integrity.

"With all due respects, Reverend, that's a bloody lie."

"Oh really, Sir, do we have to suffer your ill-mannered outbursts?"

"Ach, I want you to prove your statement!"

"So we shall. On a particular night, this February 1985, you were seen driving off with one Miss Goerzen and various Africans. You did not spend the night at home with your wife like any good Christian would. No, you passed the night in the company of this woman in the kraal of an African witch doctor. Do you deny this?"

"No, I cannot deny that I stayed at Mr. Dube's house that night and that Miss Goerzen happened to be there. That's as far as it goes. Now let me explain why I went there."

"We are not interested in any excuses that you have."

Something about the cleric's intransigence snapped the chord of Matty's control. "So, I'm guilty already. Whatever happened to your so-called civilized values you keep shouting about? I know an old African Chief who has a much higher sense of justice. I don't think you know what the word means. My only sin is that I befriended some Africans in my area."

188

Mapfumo almost gleefully shouted, "Yes, you have made very good friends with a well-known terrorist, Mr. Van der Merwe! You were seen yesterday at a township shebeen holding hands with this disreputable drunkard." Then he controlled himself lest the defence of his master became too obvious.

"So now you're the fucking CIO!" The Boer shouted and took deadly aim. In Shona, he lectured Mapfumo. "You, town man, you forget your own home training. Holding hands with a man has nothing to do with sex but has everything to do with friendship. And the so- called terrorist, Tawanda Murovi is my friend."

Mapfumo clenched his fists and was beginning to rise, but Van Rooi pushed him into his chair.

Mat continued his tirade in Afrikaans. "And you, Van Rooi, you really think I'm running around the country on my wife. That's disgusting. Besides if there was any trouble in my marriage, which there ain't, it should never be on the agenda of a Synodical Board meeting.

"Looks like you folk don't have nothing better to do than dig into a pile of manure and come up with any filth to accuse me of. That's because you don't understand what's happening in this country and what is happening to me.

"May I draw your attention to Luke 6 verse 37, before you pick out the speck from your brother's eye; make sure you take the board out of your own eye."

Mapfumo leaned back and closed his fingers into the shape of a steeple. "Now the devil is quoting scripture."

189

"Yes, and the devil has been quoting the bible for hundreds of years in this place. And I know I've been right in there quoting along with him. That's been my mistake. Yes, I've been making mistakes all my life. I have denied what my eyes keep telling me."

Van Rooi sat straighter in his seat. "And what have your eyes been telling you, Mineer?" he said with a sneer.

The innuendo was not lost on Mathias. Nor was the whole tone of these charges. "I'll tell you and I'll tell the church and the whole blerry world! I experienced more decent Christian behaviour among the blacks than I ever saw with you lot."

Someone snickered. "He's still drunk."

Mathias stood up and pointed his finger at the group. "You'd really like to think that, wouldn't you? You just gotta pick your scapegoat for the year, don't you? I have sat here and condemned people to excommunication thinking that only Hell awaited them. And now I think: why did we ever throw these people out? I'll tell you the real reasons. They were honest with themselves. They could no longer tolerate the ungodly system you're running here.

"Why is a black man shown the door when he pitches up to this church in town? Why don't you put the address of the church in the newspaper: in case a bunch of Africans show up? Why don't you want to worship beside a black man? Our schools in the communal are so decrepit yet your ministers drive fancy cars? What makes you so blerry good?

"I'll tell you something that I've suspected for a long time. You ain't good enough. You think you brought God to the heathens. Well, the African knew God long before your lot pitched up."

190

Van Rooi attempted to wear a friendly grin. To Mathias it was a death's head. "So Mr. Van der Merwe, it is now you. Why not we? You seem to forget that you are of impeccable, or shall I say, supposedly impeccably pure Afrikaner stock. Or is there some African blood in your family?"

Mathias clasped his hands to control his shaking. "You know something Reverend, for a preacher, you got a really filthy mind. You seem to think that having African blood is the worst sin for a white man. Yet the coloured problem didn't start until the first Dutch settler set foot on Cape Colony. So whose been doin' all the screwin'? Us!

"Come on now, don't look so shocked. All us chaps were told that we were baas and that included master over the black women. And we could do whatever we wanted with them. What if there might be African blood in my family; there's black blood in your own family, Reverend and it's us Afrikaners who put it there."

Every board member died a thousand times throughout Matty's tirade or prophecy, depending on whether he or she had the least sympathy with the Boer. Complete silence covered the room like a fog. Everyone's mouth was gauzed by shock.

Gone was the smile of knowing benevolence from Van Rooi's face. Instead a bony horrified man stared in disbelief at the farmer.

It was one thing for a raving black communist to say these things at some rally. It was completely another for an upright Boer to admit to the secret psychological truths of the white man's power. That power was physical and brutally applied. Religion was merely a veneer hiding this savagery from the more decent-minded. Van der Merwe's admission to the sordid methods by which a self-proclaimed superior race kept its moral sovereignty was pure treachery. And traitors like lepers must be cast out.

Van Rooi heaved with an effort to stay calm. He could not yet believe what he had heard. "As far as I am concerned, Mathias Paul Van der Merwe, you are no longer a member of this congregation. But of course, my views must be shared by a majority of the Synodical Board. But you are suspended until further notice."

"You don't have to kick me out, Reverend, I was leavin' anyway." With that, Mathias slowly walked out of the room and softly closed the door behind him.

It wasn't far from the Synod building to the place where people got lifts going out of town. Matty scuffed along the gravel edge of the road making a brave face as tears refused to go away. He was angry and appalled that he had become a sacrifice all because he had the audacity to help someone in need. *I don't blame Kindo for this serious shit.* He thought. On further reflection, he again would have sped the Makumbe family to the traditional healer on a rainy night. *If that's was the reason I'm being chased away from the church, then that church ain't worth belonging to.* Mat knew that this was true but it didn't hurt any less.

A Shu-shine bus skidded to a stop. With other passengers Matty climbed up and sat in an empty place beside a woman with her baby. The puzzled conductor looked at him.

"Where to?"

"Happy Valley turn-off."

"That's one hundred and sixty dollars,

Comrade." Mat gave him a two-dollar note, leaned back and tried to sleep.

Betty had busied herself with lunch to keep her mind off his cryptic phone call that she received at nine-thirty that morning. One thing about Mat was that he always called if he was going to be late. She tried to listen to the background noises for any clue to his location.

As she marinated the fillets, the screen door squeaked on its hinges. She slowly put down the meat and nervously walked into the living room wiping her hands on a tea towel. For the first time ever, she noticed her wrinkled and veiny hands; a farmer's wife never had nice hands. Had he come to tell her that it was over? Of course, he would pay alimony properly. Mat was like that, very decent. But she couldn't bear the years of loneliness holding the fort at her parent's place in Bulawayo. How would she explain her single presence to the crowd at the club?

Betty stopped in the middle of the room. He looked awful, unshaven, heavy-eyed and sweaty. It seemed that he walked in the noon heat for miles.

"Luv," he said, "you better sit down."

"It is coming," she thought. She girded her loins for devastation. Yet the expected words did not come.

"Betty, I've been kicked out of the church."

This was unbelievable. He didn't want to leave her after all. She was so relieved that the significance of his words did not register.

"What's that Mat?"

He mournfully looked at her. "I said, I was thrown out of the church. You know, excommunicated."

"Oh, thank God."

"Eh?" Her lightened mood confused him.

"I'm sorry darling, that's terrible. But I thought when you phoned me all secret like, you wanted to leave me."

He came over to her on the sofa and held her. "Oh God, never, never, never. If I didn't have you to come home to; I don't know what I'd do."

"Mat, I was afraid that all that gossip was half true and that you wanted to run away with that young woman. You've been acting so undercover lately."

"I wasn't hiding from you. I was just being cautious after you told me that those busybodies were flapping their tongues about me.

"Betty, I want to warn you that things are going to get pretty rough. Van Rooi and his gang chucked me off because they think I was running around on you. But that ain't the real reason and we both know that. I was so afraid that you'd leave me with the way folks seem to pick me for their spicy news for the year. It's not going to be nice for you at all. Do you still want to stay after all this?"

"You know I'll go through a burning lake with you." She pulled away from him to look into his eyes. "But we have a lot of sorting out to do, you and I."

He took her hand. "Betty, I was in jail last night. The cops got me while I was going out of town. They impounded the Ford and I have to go to court to answer drunk driving charges. That's the short and long of it."

"You were drunk then."

"Ja."

"Mat, I have never gotten cross with you for drinking but now it's become too much. You're getting into too much trouble because of booze. And I'm getting very worried about you."

"Those chaps at the club drink just as much as the chaps at Chose, you know."

"I didn't mean that you shouldn't see them. Don't be so selfish with your friends. Why don't you bring them round to the house? I'm saying cut down on the drink."

'I think we had this conversation before."

"Yis," she said crisply. "And I don't see any improvement."

Mathias hung his head. "The past year's been rough on me, luv. Maybe the worst is over."

"I hope so for both our sakes," she pursed her lips then sighed.

Chapter 16   The Party

"Hey guys, we need to celebrate," announced Debbie at Mai Nyasha's shop one weekend afternoon.

"Is there any other reason for skanking except for skanking?" Kindo began a little toe dance at the slug game.

"There is. I just got a letter today from the head creep at the Club. I am now chucked off as an undesirable guest!" Everybody whistled and cheered.

"Is it because of me," Chafichu asked.

"Don't worry about it. It's done."

Manasseh broke in. "What did you have in mind? A party?"

"Why not? I'll organize some meat and rice and we'll get a crate for three. You chaps bring your own sounds and we'll jive."

"Beautiful, let's start now!" Chafichu jumped on an empty beer crate and started a fast rhumba. His new girlfriend, Felicity bent over in stitches watching him.

Debbie laughed and twirled her finger around the side of her head. Kindo and Felicity mimicked her and Murovi slowed down.

"Don't break the crate, Tawanda. I'll tell Mai Nyasha first." She leaned over the counter and shouted into the depths of the store. "Hey, *pamusoroi,* Mai!"

The matron of the shop emerged from the bubbling chibuku room. They bought two crates of beer and two kilograms of meat for the eight men and women who happened to be there. Predictably, more folks would pitch up at Debbie's house as the news spread. Just in case Mai Nyasha put three more crates on ice.

Kudakwashe volunteered to be the deejay and Manasseh the beer master. Within two hours most of the Choselites had assembled in her living room. Wild Bill Fox, Debbie's friend, who patched things up with Johnny, happened to be at the school sorting out a donation of science supplies with Johnny.

Felicity also taught junior science and came to the lab to help with the division of supplies and tell the Canadians about the party at Debbie's. Bill insisted that Johnny come along, let bygones be bygones.

More crates were bought as the moon began to ride above the mango orchard. A bonfire was lit in the back yard to roast the meat and boil the rice and soup.

After dinner had been cleared away and the others began to dance and drink, Tawanda beckoned Debbie outside. They sat beside the fire.

Tawanda pulled a cigarette from behind his ear and lit it with a glowing twig. He began to puff.

"Hey, shamwari, did I thank you for the other time at the club?"

"That was a year ago. But I didn't do much; just one sentence and the whole universe came crashing down. You know I'm being kicked out because I don't like the word boy being applied to any man."

"Does getting chucked off disturb you so much?" He queried.

"Yes and no. No because all those assholes, I mean the white ones, are people I would never hang around with at home. If I don't move around with narrow minded, middle aged idiots in Canada, why should I do so here? So I'm not going to have heart attacks over any lost friendships, except for the Africans who work at the mine. Okay, I admit, I'll miss the movies, swimming pool and squash courts."

"But you can meet them in the village."

"I know that."

"Are stupid Hollywood movies and a squash court so important to your life?" He countered.

"No, that's not the real reason. I'm disturbed because of what they did to you and I wasn't fair or right."

"But that is typical of their kind of evil. If you want to stay with us here, you have to realize that there is a good side and an ugly side. You can't stay on the fence forever. I don't think you are anyway."

"It's just what happened after Tom did his number on you was so wrong and so wrong headed. How can otherwise rational people support such a loser?" She persisted.

"He is white, that's how."

"Then independence means nothing if these attitudes are allowed to persist."

"Oh, but it does! Nowadays my future is no longer determined by the whims of a Boer. A Boer may influence my future, but he no longer has any power over it. We Africans are now free to make our own mistakes and solve our own problems.

"The revolution." Tawanda shook his head sadly. "Ah, what revolution? It may not even come in my lifetime because we are seeking the bucks. We want to live like white men. No, any real revolution is not started by the gun. It must start in the head. I can shoot 10,000 Rhodesian soldiers but that means nothing if I become one of them. It will be a long time before we dismantle this system of Babylon. You know what de Rastas say? The system traps us then sucks out our soul, our culture everywhere: in the school, on our farms and in the ghetto.

"Ya, deception. You know, Debbie, it is healthier to get deceived by an African. He is our brother and we understand his motives. We can never be fooled by a black man for long. Why do you think there are so many coups in Africa? Don't worry about Drinkwater and his stupid friends. Leave them alone."

"But they're still my people. We have common cultural bonds."

"Rubbish," he interrupted. "You just finished telling me that you had nothing in common with them."

"Oh shit, I didn't mean it the way it sounded. You have never had to make this choice, this horrible choice. I feel like my guts are being torn apart."

"And what is so disastrous about African culture?" Tawanda was annoyed.

"Nothing, nothing at all," She pondered. "In traditional times, your people never had jails or locked up the mentally ill like we did.

"Remember that time at Mai Ruka's pub when that crazy guy in tatters was laying on the ground in the sun and begging for beer? Everyone was so patient with him. And I remember one guy took him into the shade before he got sunstroke. Later one of his relatives led him home."

Tawanda was startled, "Ya, I recall that one also. It makes me very sad; that mentally disturbed beggar used to be my commander in this area. The war made him insane. The elders say that if you kill too many people, you go crazy."

"I'm sorry about that, Chafich. I just wanted to let you know that wouldn't happen on the street in Toronto: someone would have called a cop or worse. We *marungu* have so much to learn from you. But I am not an African. I never will be. I will always be a foreigner."

"No one is asking you to stop being a Canadian. We Africans are only asking you to act in such a way that we can trust you, that you won't fix us when it's convenient for you. We ask for loyalty. You know that means risking any trust that the whites ever had in you."

She didn't like this conversation at all. In fact, it was getting dangerous because he was straining her moral fibre. He demanded a commitment that she was afraid to give.

"Listen, Tawanda, you were always black. The decision came to you as easily as learning how to tie your shoes." Her pleas dissolved into the waiting darkness.

"You are very wrong, Debbie. Don't you know there are white blacks and black blacks? When you live under an oppressive regime, it's almost natural that you identify with the oppressors. A black can become baasboy. He is baas because he wields power over his brothers and sisters. And he is boy because he is always under the whites; either under his thumb or in his pocket.

"It is never easy to make a choice; I found it very hard to side with my people."

"When you decided to become a comrade?"

"Yes," and he fell silent.

"Tawanda, I've known you for over two years. You joke a lot about killing the Rhodies but you really don't talk about it. I've noticed that with genuine comrades: they never really talk about the war at all. Why is that?"

"Because it hurts. We remember the horrors, the uncertainty and the bitterness of war. Sometimes I wake up at night and I still think I'm in the forest." In a softer tone, he almost whispered, "Sometimes I even see the faces of the soldiers I killed. Sometimes they visit me in my dreams at night." He was quiet for a long moment. Then he steadied himself and resumed his story.

"We went over the border with stars in our eyes. We were fighting the capitalist exploiter. We were the Vanguard of the Revolution. But when we got to the bush and saw the suffering of our people -- ah, believe you me, *ChiMuti* made them suffer more because of us -- I began to understand that I was fighting for my mother and father so that they could be first class citizens in the land of our ancestors, our own country. Forget about socialism. We wanted to study and work because of our talents not because we wanted to become white." He sighed tiredly.

"Who is ChiMuti, again?"

"Little tree, Ian Smith. Ah, when I think about that guy! Ccl. He was taking lessons in cruelty from the South Africans. We were badly off but, *mai we,* those people down there are in deep trouble. Those Transvaal Boers are hard core cruel.

"I was beginning to tell you that my decision was not as easy as you might think. I nearly became a baasboy. I nearly went to Britain to study. I nearly became one of those who ran away like *tsuro* the hare and then return back to get the big job when the smoke cleared. Notice the word nearly. But that didn't happen.

"You know my father worked under the Cold Storage Commission. He even became an auctioneer. We kids always went to school in clean and good clothes. We always had plenty of food. There were always school fees. I really didn't know how lucky I was until the war.

"In 1975 my parents told me to stay at Gokomere whilst I was doing my A-levels because the war was getting pretty hot in Chivi. Before I finished, I applied for a place at the local university. This was denied because they said their quota for African students doing Shona and History was filled. I was a number, just another fuzzy head in the classroom. I wasn't even the human being Tawanda Murovi, who got straight A's in History, English Literature, Shona and General Paper, the best results in the province. You can understand that I was extremely bitter.

"And what does a bright boy like me do? He applies for a scholarship overseas. If the Rhodesians wouldn't have me, I knew the British would. The best mistake of my life was to go home because I had not seen my mother for over a year.

"In August 1976 Mai was cooking for the

comrades. The Boys were there on the night I walked home from the road. We were in a semi-liberated area and I had to trek 15 kilometres off the tarmac. The moon was full that night and I was frightened of soldiers.

"Comrade Grenade who was sober in those days, he was seated in the yard talking to my mother when I pitched up. All through the night he lectured me, convincing me that I could study any time. Now was the time to fight.

"You know when I see Grenade nowadays, it makes me very sad. He was my commander in the early days before I was assigned to my area of operation. Now he is another drunken beggar like poor Comrade Africa, the chap we saw at Mai Ruka's. Except Grenade is still in his right mind but he has no job."

"That's nobody's fault, Tawanda. He did that to himself."

"I know, but it doesn't make it any less tragical. I can say more about Grenade but that is also a long story. The next morning, I told my mother that I was leaving. She asked where. I told her Mozambique. She was upset but not very surprised.

"You know I was in the bush for six months sleeping in caves and on leaves before I realized that this wasn't Tawanda Murovi against the Boers. It was my people's war. Without them, we would lose. I grumbled because I couldn't go to university. Most people grumbled because they couldn't get clinics or education or even clothes.

"Ah, my people were poor in those days. One bottle of orange squash was the big Christmas treat.

Peasant farmers wore animal skins because they were too poor. Yet they fed us when we starved; clothed us when the Guti wind froze our blood and gave us their own huts with reed mats. Man, that was paradise compared to the forest!" His natural good humour broke the mood and he nudged Debbie.

"You know what I bought with my first demobilization pay?" He chuckled. "A bed! A nice double bed with a very comfortable mattress. I didn't care if Chafichu had any place to PUT the thing. Even the middle of Baker Ave. in Harare would be fine. But I was determined that I was going to sleep on my own new bed." He laughed loud and long.

Debbie could imagine the irrepressible Chafichu hauling his double bed into the chamber of parliament. Laying back and taking a long pull at a quart of Lion, he would announce to the legislators. "Comrade Speaker, sorry to interrupt your deliberations, but Comrade Chafichu needs some place to put his bed!"

Again, he grew serious. "Sorry I got off topic. My point is that I had to make a choice between running and fighting. I am quite clear now but I was only nineteen then. I was a boy. At least your choice is easier. You don't have to live here forever. Do you know what I mean?"

"You mean Matty Van der Merwe."

"Exactly. That man is in serious shit."

"How, he's not getting kicked out of the Club," she muttered.

"Debbie sometimes I think you are too stubborn for nothing. It is much harder for him to come on the black side."

"I know that. If he weren't raised in such a sick society, he'd be an excellent man."

"He may be yet. Something very bad happened to him in town the other week."

"What?"

"He spent the night in a cell. His truck was arrested too. You see, after the stock sale he came to Tafara Beer Hall and got stinking drunk with us. I and Kindo were skanking with some Chivi brethren. Matty bought us a lot of beer. And I thought: if miracles can happen, this is it. But miracles exact a very dear price. The police got him on the Mutare road. There was a church meeting the next morning and Murimi we Mombe was seriously *babalazi* for the occasion. A reliable source told me that he said that he was no longer interested in their apartheid system and I quote, 'the ungodly system you're running here.'

"They chucked him from the congregation in town. He has lost the protection of his Afrikaner God. And he cannot run to Canada or Britain. He has no place left to go but to my people. And we love him because he has suffered on our account."

"He can always recant. Tawanda, he's fifty-three. He'll be a very lonely old man someday. But then again, remember the first time we met him at my house when he was torturing his Kombi?"

"Well, to tell the truth, Debbie, I kind of met him during the war, but I was in the darkness standing guard when Ambuya Chitombo warned him and his wife to leave before the action started in his place.

"But I recollect the time in your house. Hah, was that only a year ago?" Tawanda shook his head.

205

"Hm. Well, as he was leaving with his fixed tire I told him about Beyers Naude who gave up everything to work for the Africans. Maybe something sunk in." She explained.

Tawanda continued. "You know old woman Chitombo practically raised Matty Dread. She breastfed him because his mother died when he was a small baby. Kudakwashe told me. Many of the older Boers are like that."

Debbie thought about those depression years before antibiotics when many women died soon after they gave birth. "So that's why he can speak Shona like peasant farmer."

"Exactly. And Boers are very stubborn. Mat will never apologize for what he has done and said. You must understand something about the Afrikaner. They are bastards but they are honest bastards. Murimi is an honest Boer and he is a good one because he told his people the truth about what they are. And you must help him, Debbie."

"Ah no, no ways! What am I supposed to do: conduct racial relations classes for repentant Rhodies?"

"Don't be too funny. You know what I mean. You expatriates can help people like Matty Dread live together properly with Africans. You are always bragging about your democratic traditions. Show the white Zimbabwean how to achieve this. Your culture trains you how to behave properly with different peoples."

"Not exactly. Treating a person as his or her

humanity requires without prejudice is a struggle that I have to deal with. There's racism and classism in not so

206

pure little Canada, you know. Don't take me as an example for all of us. Look at John; he's a more typical first world, two-faced jerk."

Tawanda laughed. "I like your English." He threw a dried msassa log on the fire. "You are what Canada can produce. John's problem is that he wants to be all things to all men: the great development worker, while still the great friend of the baas. A person cannot do that here."

"This is true," she agreed. "One has to work from a central ideology. A person's acts must be consistent with her words. And I'm having a heck of a time achieving that in my life." Debbie confessed.

"All human beings who think about what they do have trouble with that one. Now what did Shakespeare say? 'To thine own self be true, therefore you cannot be false with any man.' I think that's how it goes. Anyways, Hamlet Act 2 Polonius' speech."

"Iwe, you are a scholar. I thought that was from one of the Henrys."

"But do you understand what I mean about decisions and their consequences?" Having confessed some of his soul, Tawanda studied her intently waiting for her reply.

"I do," she said finally. "I don't like it but I read you loud and clear. If I escape now, the CHOICE will follow me wherever I go. That's why I like and dislike talking to you, Tawanda. You dissect me."

"Use the word stimulate, it's less brutal." He searched the thigh pocket of his trousers for another cigarette.

She looked up at the Southern Cross. "Yeah, I need a long time to think. If it weren't for the party, I would go off to a rock some place and meditate."

"Go and do it." He urged. "Manasseh is a good beer master and Kuda won't destruct your stereo. Since I am security chief, I will prevent all fights."

"Hah, you mean you'll start them."

"Come on, Sissy, I promise. I am a man of my word. Absolutely no performances by Chafichu unless necessary. Besides, Felicity is here to protect me from myself."

"Hm. I wonder if I'll have a house left." She began to chuckle.

"Trust me." He winked hugely.

She answered him in Shona. "Okay, little brother, let me get my walking stick,"

He didn't see her go out the door and down the path to the village, to find a quiet rock to think. But he knew which transcendent landscapes she would travel that night. He trekked the same route nine years before: an anxious boy hurrying along the mountain paths to Chimoio, Mozambique.

At times like these, Murovi felt very close to his ancestors. *He had revealed so much of himself to a foreigner and this was very confusing. Had she discerned the real issue? Could he trust her? He needed*

their guidance. Churches were alien places to be avoided. Even the traditional ceremonies at home in Chivi seemed less than spontaneous. But God, the Creator of the Whole World, the Almighty, showed

208

Himself in the fragrance of the jacaranda, the fervent growth of maize. He was always there, never to be shunned or compartmentalized. Murovi's forefathers were very wise when they said that a human being was far too ignorant to speak directly to Mwari. A man needed his ancestors to intercede for him. For one who had lived too close to death, eternity was only a thought away. Prophets were the only ones who could give us focused glimpses of the Plan.

As the fire waned he got down on his haunches in traditional supplication, clapped hands and poured beer on the ground. He began to speak to them in the rich tones of the ancient stone mason/warrior/ priest.

"Grandfather and Great Grandfather, I hope you are resting well. This is your son Tawanda, son of Samuel, son of Tinashe of the Lion Totem from the Chieftainship of Chivi. Please accept my poor offering of white man's beer. That is all I have and my need is great. I thank you for all the help you have given to me and my generation to achieve what we have.

"If you are willing, can you take this question to the elder ancestors, for I am a small boy and do not know how to talk to the Almighty. Can our elders please ask Him: Does our liberation mean the liberation of the white man? Is this part of the scheme: that hatred should turn to love and prejudice to compassion? Please help me to understand and guide my actions; for I am not wise enough. I am now finished. My forefathers, rest in peace." He clapped his hands to complete the petition.

At what price was freedom won? For Tawanda the missing children and absent mothers seemed very high. He mourned for the dead of his family and of his clan. He even felt pity for the whites because he had killed their sons. And now the Chefs in the big cities

209

reaped what was not sown by them. The price paid by the fallen seemed exorbitant. He was bitterly grieved. When would it begin to hurt less, he wondered.

She saw him hunched over the fire and knew he was talking to the ancestors. Felicity stepped quietly to the log and waited for him to finish. She saw the open suffering on her lover's face. "Tawanda, is there anything wrong?" She asked gently.

One never pried too far into another's thoughts; for they were the African's only private possessions. Even for lovers and spouses, one never pried unless invited to do so. They sat quietly together watching the fire. "Tawanda, I need to sleep early."

"Oh, I thought you were coming to my place tonight."

"Maybe you can come to my house but it can't be too late. I need to get to the bus station at 7 o'clock with my sister. I'm taking her to Gokomere for an interview to enter A-Levels. She passed her entrance exam."

Chafichu was thrilled for her "Congratulations, Feli, she is smart girl and will do well there."

"You like the *VaRomas* at Gokomere?"

"Sure, I passed out of my A-levels there in 1976. I had good teachers and the Jesuits love we Africans and they are fair with all the students." He replied.

"That's good news, Chafich. Don't be too late. I will leave the key in the basket by the door." She kissed him good night.

Unsteady footsteps intruded into their space. "Hey Murovi, let's skank, man."

Then Kindo saw the woman leaving, "Am I disturbing something?"

"It's all right, blas. Felicity is taking her sister to Gokomere tomorrow morning. Let's drink!" The transformation from petitioner to boyfriend to Chafichu was complete. Forget your weakness and dance. Forget your troubles and dance. They swayed arm in arm into the pulsating party.

Chapter 17   Babalazi Blues

"Jesus H Christ, Chafichu, you look awful!"

A very dishevelled Murovi wove dipsomaniacal patterns at Debbie's front door at exactly nine am. The sun shone cruelly.

"I'm still drunk, of course. He tried one of his expansive gestures and nearly fell sideways. His lower lip stuck out half a meter and profuse lacerations decorated his puffy face.

Just outside the door freshly scrubbed, lilac - scented ladies gaily paraded to church. The brighter than white starched blouses and turbans set off by deep sable skirts made Debbie's bleary eyes ache.

"Get in here, you numbskull!" She dragged Chafichu through the door and shut out the leering daylight. "You really want the reverend to swoop down on you, don't you? And then you'll have a nice excuse to perform a blasphemy in front of the church ladies!"

"Ah sissy Debbie, are you angry with me too?" He wheedled petulantly. "I tried to joke with some of the chaps in front of their houses this morning but they said, 'Ah no, Chafichu. You behaved poorly last night.' They did not even invite me inside; they ignored me." His face screwed up as if he were about to cry or break furniture. Instead he staggered across the room and slumped into a chair. Debbie stood fists in her hips and ready to rumble. She glared at him.

"Chafichu, against my better judgement, I actually feel sorry for you. But I'm very pissed off at you. And I will give you four reasons why."

He shot daggers at her.

"Iwe, you wait a minute. Number one: you're an a- hole. Number two: you have the unique talent for single handedly wrecking my party, which in this case was turning out to be a great party."

"So, Comrade Professor, if you are now finished..."

"I'm not finished. Number three: you beat up a guest of mine."

"And what am I: the message boy, the garden boy?"

"Don't be funny for nothing. You were also a guest of mine. And you and this other person ruined the peace of my house.

"All right, Johnny is a stuck up, racist creep. My lurking suspicions were confirmed last night. But he was welcome in my house as you were. And I don't expect two colleagues of mine to pound the shit out of each other in my living room. I also don't expect my guests to smash my glassware."

"What glasses? You're mad." At this point he was up and weaving grotesquely.

"Check the slivers on the floor and watch out for the broken beer bottles. Why did you tear up my books in your drunken fury? Notice the word MY. Since when is it African tradition to destroy your friend's house because you're having an argument with a third party? How is my innocent copy of *Petals of Blood* involved in this?"

Tawanda's face began to twitch.

"Number four: ah, don't interrupt with any revolutionary crap. I am not in the mood this morning. Number four: Johnny is not my friend. Get that in capital letters, NOT MY FRIEND! If he came here today, I would have told him to fuck off. And you know I don't use the f word often. This is how furious I am with both of you.

"But you are my friend, Tawanda. That's why I let you in. Even though my countryman's blood is till on your t- shirt, I let you in. And you better make it good."

Her white-hot indignation more than her logic, stunned him. He fell into the same chair, pulled his dust smeared beret over his eyes and mumbled.

"I never thought ... No forget that one. How you could think... nah, that one's useless...I mean... I have better home training than this. My father ... never in his house would I dare..."

"So what makes you think you can act like a baboon in mine?"

"Debbie, please. I am a proud man and ... apologies are very hard for me."

Her natural kindness reasserted itself when she saw his dejected figure in the chair and she shook her head. She asked more amiably. "Do you want some coffee or tea? Well the kettle's on and I was just making breakfast when you, ah, knocked. How's sausages and eggs?"

Mollified, he said, "Ya, I'm hungry. Felicity went early to Gokomere with her sister, so yes, thank you." Then a mischievous grin creased his face. "Can I have a cold one for babalazi?"

"No ways, besides there's not a drop left in the place. If there was I wouldn't give it to you."

"Ah, you are too cruel," he simpered half mockingly.

"Let me take a look at that face of yours. Tch, your lip is terrible. What part of the furniture did he schmuck you with?"

"His fist."

She was disgusted. "You friggin' men will never learn."

"Silence, woman," But his attempt was lame. "Ah, that hurts." He winced at her abrasive exploration.

"Your cuts are filthy. Come on, stick out your face."

He obeyed by sticking out his neck. Debbie slipped into the bedroom to get some methylated spirits. She padded back with cotton dripping purple liquid. Before he could escape, she dived at him.

"Ahhhhhhhhhh. Tawanda tried to roll himself into a ball, but going backwards, she succeeded in scrubbing most of the dirt out of the wounds on his face. "That hurts, man!"

"Too bad, be a man." She cackled.

"You are revenging me."

"Tut tut, infana. Would you prefer Mai Tinashe at the clinic?"

Immediately Tawanda envisioned the well-

215

known sadist in a white uniform grinding wet cotton wool into his raw flesh. He began to co-operate with Debbie's far gentler ministrations. However, she was not going to let up on the verbal assault.

"Sex and war: you men would screw and fight till you destroy the planet and leave it to the women to clean up your --- oh my God. Your gums are torn apart. Looks like we'll have to visit Mai Tinashe after all. That's unless you want those holes to fester, become abscessed and Chafichu dies of foot in the mouth disease."

"I do not like this conversation." He muttered while the ubiquitous cotton scrubbed away the scabs and grit inside his mouth.

"You should have thought of that when you were pounding Johnny's head against a wall."

"You saw that?" The punishment was over and he could talk.

"I saw more. When I came from my walk, I heard all kinds of shouting. I came in the door at the same time you and Johnny went flying across the table pounding at each other while the bottles and cutlery smashed. It was worse than *The Return of Shanghai Joe* because the crazy fight happened in MY HOUSE in peaceful little Dhuma village. And I thought I was hallucinating.

"When Kindo and Kuda finally managed to pull you two apart, I couldn't make any sense out of either of you, being so drunk and so insane. Do you remember any of it?"

"Ya, most of it. But I'm getting hungry."

"You mean you don't want to talk about it."

"Not now." He pleaded.

"Okay, temporary truce."

Shortly after, a well fed, cleaner and soberer Chafichu sat quietly in Debbie's VW Bug and the unwanted memory of the night before preyed on his mind.

"Yer awfully quiet, Chafich."

"Ya, I'm trying to understand how I could come to blows like that over beer talk."

"What happened?"

"Ah, it started off innocently enough. I and Bill were jiving."

"How did Bill and Johnny get here?"

"Bill was in the lab with Johnny and Felicity went to help them with the supplies. She told them about the party and they came. Things were skanking beautifully until Jay said something about Bill turning gay. Well I left it because I didn't know what Jay was talking about.

And I was about to ignore it when Bill said that Jay was full of shit. "In Zimbabwe, the girls dance with the girls and the boys dance with the boys."

"Then Johnny said something like only in the reserves. And Bill said, "It's the majority that rules here, buddy." I remember that very clearly. Then I remember the next part even worse.

"Johnny said, 'don't tell me that you're swallowing that rah-rah Mugabe shit.'

217

"I didn't like that statement so I tried to explain a few things like Cde. Mugabe was my Commander and Chief. You know one drunkard should never try to correct another drunkard. He just shot daggers at me and shouted, 'Chafichu, fuck off. This is none of your business!'

"Iwe," I said. You are doing down my country and culture. And I don't like what you say about Cde. Mugabe.

"Then Johnny got hot and scolded me. He said, 'Who the fuck do you think you are, shorty?'

"You know I fought some men as big as Johnny and they were bush hard Boers. Since Jay was soft, I could destruct him easily."

Debbie was not satisfied. "Well?"

"I don't like to be pushed away. *Saka*, I called him some rude names and he called me others. Then we started pushing and pushes became punches.

"When you came in, things were getting serious. Tell me, Debbie. Why are you and Bill so different from Johnny?"

"For the same reasons that the government isn't socialist enough for you and the reverend is a creature of the Synod. Remember last night you told me about white Africans and black Boers?"

"Maybe Johnny took a walk and decided to go on the other side," he conjectured.

"Probably," she said churlishly because the minimal respect she had for Johnny disappeared.

218

"Speaking of Boers, I collected from a reliable source that you are having an affair with Murimi." He grinned painfully.

Debbie howled so loud she nearly stalled the car. "Iwe, his stomach is too big. It'd cramp our style."

"How do you know his stomach his soft?"

"Tawanda, you really are a menace," she giggled.

"Come on, sissy, let's have an affair. I don't have a stomach at all."

"No ways, Number 1, Felicity is a friend of mine and I think she would cream me in a fight. Number 2, if you keep boozing, your gut will be as big as Matty Dread's. Besides sex is a wonderful way to wreck our friendship. After the big mutual orgasm, we'd have to rediscover each other all over again."

He grinned sheepishly and looked between his knees.

"Come on, Tawanda, does this really embarrass you?" She was surprised.

"Slightly." He breathed easier hoping that she would change the topic.

"Sorry, you'll have to excuse us North Americans. For the last twenty years, we've been talking about sex to even our house plants."

"Maybe we Africans don't talk about it enough."

"No, Tawanda, don't change that part of you. Modesty is refreshing after the flesh mags and sex shops of my own country."

219

"But you must remember that town blacks can be very obscene. I guess I'm still a villager at heart because I don't like their rude talk especially in front of women."

"That's the part of Zimbabwe that I love. You know old man Chakurira?"

"Sure."

"He reminds me of my grandfather, a really straight-laced Mennonite farmer who wouldn't say shit if his mouth was full of it."

Chafichu slapped his knee in delight. "Hah, I love that English of yours."

"Dialect, sweetie, dialect. I remember I said shit in front of him one time and he said. 'Ja, it's twenty dollars a ton.' Maybe I understand the old man better now."

"Well, Debbie, I don't want you to change either. Here is the clinic." He groaned in anticipation of renewed suffering.

Meanwhile at the more sophisticated mine clinic, Johnny lay moaning on the table while the nurse sewed up the corner of his left eye. He had driven there alone with his bitter thoughts.

Chapter 18   Ambuya

It was past midnight and an eagle owl swooped over the moonlit hills. Hard-silvery light sparkled on the innocuous grey rocks as if ice crystals had lodged into the fault lines. The stubble fields of decapitated maize stalks rustled in the faint wind. Beyond the empty fields, and before the sylvan bulk of Zimunya Mountain, the family plot of Kudakwashe's grandmother's people lay in a surprisingly lush bowl of land in the shadow of the feared mountain.

Into its borders, long ago, a wily, vengeful wizard fled the homicidal mobs from a beer drink. Earlier in the evening a guest stumbled upon the wizard as he was crushing some lethal leaves into a powder. He was waiting for the ripe moment to kill ten people with one dash. The elders said that the people ran him down under the eaves of the forest and cut him into pieces. They fed the meat to the owls. The area was a fit place for graves but rather an anxious one for the living guardians of the deceased.

Three days previously an urgent phone call pulled Kudakwashe out of a form four class room. While haranguing the students, he prowled the rows like an avenging lion nipping at the heels of scattering gazelles.

"Boys and girls," he boomed, "sometimes I think you are not normal. How many thousands of times have I told you that your disgusting English will cause you to fail more than English Language? You seem immune to any correction. You tear up your test papers as if my red marks carried AIDS. Of course, I don't expect you to understand a single word I am saying because you do not want to practise English, as if the white man's language will give you leprosy." Unlike the more fortunate gazelles, the students could not run away immediately.

221

"Foolish children! If you do not practise English and pass Language you will not get a job! " In the middle of his temper tantrum, which he sarcastically labelled 'common errors' in the scheme book, there was a furious pounding on the door. This announced a self-important prefect bruising his knuckles to make sure he was heard. The cocky senior lost his bubble as soon as he saw the murderous look on his teacher's face. The boy trembled and shrank back.

"Excuse me, Suh, there is a phone for you."

Kuda fumed, "Speak sense, boy! Repeat: there is a telephone call for you."

Predictably the student was too intimidated to speak for the next ten seconds. But Kuda's raised fist urged verbalization.

Timidly, "There is a telephone call for you, Suh."

"Better." Kudakwashe smouldered and stalked across the compound like an

attacking buffalo. Half way under the grove of msassa trees, he muttered insanely against the years of frustrating and penurious toil. "Noble profession - rubbish! Better take my two-term leave and open up a bottle store and grinding mill while I'm still correct in the head!"

Chitombo cooled down by the time he reached the tiny cupboard of an administration office. Two desks, two typewriters and two fashionably dressed secretaries squeezed into the three-square meter space. The accounts books found repose in an overflowing and tattered cardboard box. He grabbed the crank phone and shouted into the receiver, as the reception in this part of the

222

province was like shouting across the football field during a hail storm.

On a spare period, Kindo lounged in the doorway expecting a barrage because he observed that his friend was in fine fettle this morning and he wasn't even babalazi. A danger sign meaning that it was time for Kuda to go on leave.

Suddenly Chitombo's body went slack and his sun blackened face began to lose colour. Kindo knew viscerally that his friend had just received some bad news. From the hysterical sobs of his mother's young sister, Kuda collected that his beloved grandmother was gone. All the irritation and anger over his job, in fact every feeling haemorrhaged from him and he became one of the walking dead. In a shock faint voice, he told Kindo, "My friend, Ambuya is dead."

Like swimmers the secretaries came to him and shook his hand saying they were sorry. The headmaster heard the customary wailing and knew that one of his staff had lost a relative. He floated into the little office and also took Kuda's hand in commiseration.

The bereaved began to make mental plans to call his wife in Gweru but his numb body would not obey. He managed to whisper, "My wife, I must call her."

"I will call her," Mr. Urozvi said kindly.

Kuda's sister, Chiedza, was hopefully doing something useful in the form three class room. His sons were similarly hunched over their scribblers in the primary school down the road. He did not want to go back to the empty house.

On a deeper level, he kept asking his ancestors:

223

Who? To an African, there was no such thing as a natural death. Kuda felt himself being gently pulled along as he and Chafichu floated past the science block to the strip tar road and down the dust lane to Murovi's house. A frosty beer was put into Kuda's hand. He was sitting in an easy chair beside his friend's stereo. Radio Three played very softly.

All that day disconnected sensations entered upon the body and mind of Kudakwashe Chitombo. A malty wetness often slid down his throat. Insipid starch moistened by equally insipid brown liquid with brown lumps filled his stomach.

Brown and white faces sadly looked his way while many hands pressed his. He did not come out of that stupor till a gibbous moon pierced through his bedroom window. He found that his senses, muscles and brain were unified once again. Kuda lay on his own bed having no idea how the time passed nor who brought him home, nor how he even undressed himself.

He felt wretchedly alone. At last a great choking sob welled up in his throat and he gave in to his grief. Presently he felt soft, strong arms encircle him and he wept almost rapturously. A sense of relief: devotedly his wife had come home.

A little later, "Mother of Tinashe, how did you come?" He asked tremulously.

She stroked him lightly and whispered. "One of my classmates was fortunately going south. Thus, he gave me a lift and he drove like a ghost was chasing him. I arrived early to town. Like a miracle your uncle's son was waiting for me at the bus rank with your dad's truck."

"Where is Grandma?"

"Farmer of Cattles brought her from Gutu Hospital to Manzunzu's home. He also killed a beast for the funeral." Kuda breathed deeply and buried his head between her breasts and cried himself to sleep.

The reputation of the deceased and the survivors has always been measured by the attendance at the funeral. Sons, grandsons and granddaughters who worked or studied in far places like Harare and Bulawayo made the long journey to Chisungo. In the week before her death the old woman told her son, Rungamai, that she wanted to lie beside her ancestors in Chisungo. She was one of Dhuma's people before she married the tough and proud Majira named Chitombo.

Above all other women, Kuda loved his grandmother. He lived with her during three of his primary grades and all of his secondary education when his mother worked in town to earn more cash to pay school fees for their growing family. It was from Ambuya that he learned who his father's people were: the retainers of an ancient king. He found out that in 1896 his great grandfather was one of the soldiers of the confederation of Majiras, Zimutos and Shumbas who gallantly pitted their futile spears and assegais against the guns of the British South Africa company. Kudakwashe felt that his own gun running and spying for the comrades during the second liberation war paled in comparison.

He was morosely glad that half of Gutu and everybody who was somebody in Chisungo showed up. All the farm labourers from Happy Valley and unobtrusively, Mr. and Mrs.Van der Merwe also appeared. Hundreds of mourners sat under the few trees or in the May sunshine and quietly listened to the eulogy given by the reverend from Chose Mission.

Next the assembly followed the pall bearers in their circuit of Manzunzu's compound so that the soul could look at its earthly home for the last time. On the first anniversary of the funeral, another ceremony would be held to call the spirit home from its wandering.

Then the long walk to the family plot ensued. The bared heads of the men and the covered heads of the women were bent. Any other time much voluble chatter would have emanated from such a large crowd, but now only scuffing feet and a continuous haze of dust disturbed the observant silence.

All the teachers from Chose (except for Johnny) walked in a group. There were also about one hundred students. Though Kuda was a tough school master, he was fair and taught in earnest. His pupils secretly loved him. Directly behind the Manzunzu and Chitombo families walked Mat and Betty Van der Merwe. Mat remembered her *as the kind young black woman who nursed him, the only mother he had known since his own mother died when he was a baby. She taught him her language and told him old stories as he sat in her hut with his friend Rungamai, who now was also an old man bent over in grief.*

In her gentle way, Ambuya Chitombo had touched many lives with her quiet wisdom. Matty's heart was sore and tears streamed down his red cheeks. After all that had happened to him in the past year; he now understood that with his old nanny's death, a part of himself was gone.

The long line finally came to rest at the already dug grave. The relatives and friends who volunteered for the job had their pant legs rolled up. Periodically a young girl came with a bucket of clear water to pour on the sides of the pit. It is believed that the dust from the grave is

226

harmful to the living. The hole was at least two meters deep. First the grandsons took the old woman's sleeping mat and laid it first on the bottom of the pit. Then the black coffin, made by a local carpenter, was lowered by ropes. One by one the mourners came to say good bye to Ambuya. Each had a handful of dirt which he or she dropped into the hole. Sun baked bricks were then cemented over the box.

This was to make sure that the dead were not disturbed by any witches who would want to use the limbs for *sandawana*. Otherwise the witches would carry off the corpse and make medicine from it to kill people.

After the whole coffin was covered by bricks, tons of earth were shovelled into the hole, making sure that the dust never reached the diggers. Matty began to join in the effort but the Chose headmaster dragged him off. "Murimi, you cannot do this."

"Why not?" Mathias was crushed. He wanted to do something to prevent his grief form overwhelming him.

"Murimi," Urozvi placated him. "This is a young man's work. We know how much you loved Ambuya. But you are an old man and you must be patient."

Chafichu and Kindo were taking stones from a wheel-barrow and placing them on top of the mound. Small stones gave way to boulders which would eventually make a cairn. It would be to this pile of stones that succeeding generations would come to pour beer for Ambuya and here these descendants would pray for rains and plead for her intercession in their troubled lives.

sandawana – evil magic

227

On the night of the burial, a vigil was kept for the repose of the dead and to guard the remains from witches. Predictably Chafichu and Kindo joined Kuda and the other male relatives that night. Women were not allowed this privilege.

Predictably, the guardians came well prepared with freshly brewed rapoko beer, meat to roast over the fire and three crates of Castle. The owl's eerie hooting grew fainter as it swooped and circled Zimunya Mountain and its cries were swallowed by a gaping vale between the hills. The three friends huddled closer to the small flame. Strewn on the ground nearby were about three dozen empties. The home brew had disappeared long before. So had the other relatives. Both Chitombos and Manzunzus had returned to their more comfortable beds on some pretext of having to return to work on the next day or that the night caused the flu.

"Ccl, those cowards devoured the meat and guzzled the beer." Kuda growled. The mass desertion had put him once again into a foul mood.

Kindo nudged Chafichu and exclaimed in the serious tones of a medical practitioner. "Comrade Doctor, it appears that the patient is returning to his bad-tempered but normal self."

Kindo's esteemed colleague concurred. "Evidently, my dear Makumbe. Your prescription of one crate a day has proved effective."

Kuda rumbled in the bottom of his throat. "Look here, chaps; I don't like staying here as much as you do. But I have to, don't I." He peered at the inseparables who were secretly grinning into the timid flames. "Ah, chaps I should not get angry with you."

"That's better, Majira. Now you have to be sociable or we don't accept your apology." Chafichu pressed on him a full pint which had become quite chilled. The frosty nights of winter were not far off.

Kindo threw some more thick sticks on the fire. The flames licked at the chilly air and cast shadows on the cairn nearby. "Come on Kuda, tell us a good one so we won't. I mean to say that...there are a lot of ghosts around here."

"Ah, don't worry about spirits, Kindo" Chafichu punctuated his remark with a swig from his bottle. "I intend to get nicely drunk and sleep on those stones. That's if Grandma doesn't mind. You see I can sleep peacefully and watch the grave at the same time. I will be able to feel it if some witch wants to tap the tomb."

Kuda had shifted his position about three times in the past ten seconds. "Tch. Chafichu, I don't like that statement. Talk about something else, please."

A low delicious laugh rose from the depths of Chafichu's light frame. He boomed and cackled and slapped his thigh. "Headmasters!"

Kuda shook his head and Kindo giggled. "What headmasters?

"You know this one in town was hitting his teachers."

Always one for precision, Chitombo asked. "You mean some senile fool was beating his teachers? I have heard of such things. Especially down down in places like. Nyajena, these mentally disturbed dictators with their standard seven educations have actually caned temporary teachers!"

"No no, I mean the other kind of hit," Murovi smiled wickedly.

"Oh, you mean put."

"Ya, that's it."

Kindo was getting restive. "I just don't know how these monkeys can chase school girls and lose their jobs when there are lots of things in the beer halls."

"There are also lots of VDs in the pubs too." Kuda reminded him.

"No, no, comrades. This particular old man was hitted one certain female teacher." Murovi continued.

"Who?"

"Well this headmaster and his wife work at the same school. That's a secondary school in the township. Anyway, every lunch time the wife has her meal in her classroom and the chef supposedly has his in the office. This seems to be a queer arrangement but this is what I collected from a chap who teaches there.

"It seems that every day this old man and a juicy young lady go to the library and have activities together."

"Hah," Kindo laughed. "That school was not being administered because the old fool was seated in his office dreaming of how he is going to put his girlfriend. Tch."

Chafichu sniggered and continued. "One day last month the teacher in charge of the library got some books from the Regional Office. He wanted to put them into the room. What does he find when he gets inside, but the hardmaster with his trousers down and a woman, who is not his wife, with her skirts up. The old man was so busy that he didn't even notice that somebody entered.

"In about thirty seconds the whole staff was at the door shouting and here was their chef trying to pull on his trousers. His wife came in and began to beat the girlfriend. In fact, she nearly killed her. The girlfriend was in the hospital for two weeks and her husband is demanding ten thousand dollars from the headmaster or he will go to ministry. And get this: the chef has to borrow the money from his wife!"

"Jesus." Kindo laughed. "This is a very filthy story."

"Now usually when a chap is bitching, he quietly takes the woman to a hotel." Kuda sipped thoughtfully. "Of course, any intelligent man would. But I guess that chef is quite stupid. Or if he and the lady in question were both absent from school, they would have been caught earlier. I heard that this headmaster is one of those upright citizens who is the chairman of this committee and the president of that organization.

"Hah, all men play around on their wives." Kuda concluded throwing his empty near the fire. "Peace in the house depends on whether he plays recklessly or safely."

Kindo gazed at his big friend strangely. Kuda noticed the glance and started to justify himself. "Kindo, why are you surprised? Ah, yes, you have only been married for two years and your wife still lives with you. Besides, a man needs some variety in his life."

"Do you, Kuda? Makumbe asked softly.

"But isn't every man playing at one time or

231

another?" The statement was lamely delivered. Remembering the comfort that his wife had recently brought him, Kuda paced around the fire to hide his uneasiness.

Chafichu pensively gazed into the flames and said. "No, not every man. One time, before Felicity, I was moving around with Matty Dread in town. We were both extremely drunk and I suggested that we go find some nice flesh. Well he just looked at me and said it was all right for me because I was still loose. But he didn't do that sort of thing. Imagine, he has been married for over thirty years; he is rich and can afford the best, but he goes home to a wife with grey hair. What a strange man!

"Now I know for a fact that the white man hits the young ones just as much as we do. But their wives divorce them. That's the only difference. And to think those hyenas at his former church accused him of sleeping with Debbie, bastards!"

Kindo offered more information. "My wife tells me that Murimi and Mrs. Murimi are coming to Chose Church. Now they are worshipping with us."

"He has really changed, hasn't he?" Kuda surmised. "It was very generous what he did for my family. Even his wife came to the funeral."

"I saw him weeping like a small boy," said Kindo.

"It's because my grandmother raised him. That's why he speaks Shona like an African. He was very close playmates with my father until he was sent away to school to learn how to be a white man."

Chafichu mused. "Perhaps he is unlearning how to be baas and remembering how to be an African."

232

Chapter 19   Budzi Stereophenia

With long, keen sight peering down from azure heights, it soared over the village expecting to see the chief in the high place separated from the mobs of courtiers. The bird waited for the Chief to wave his sceptre for silence as his leopard skin flapped in the breeze. The spirit medium in his black and white blanket should have been trance dancing in communication with the royal spirits. Warriors, hunters and commoners should have surrounded the high place and at a discreet distance the women should have looked on with deferential awe.

But the golden fish eagle did not see the usual scene. Instead the shock horror and the impropriety of it: rows of boys and girls stood together paying attention to a woman flinging her arms from the right to the left. What was this grotesque pantomime? This woman was a mere commoner because she did not wear the special blanket of the spirit medium, nor was she a big wife of the chief.

Ah, there he is the descendent of Dhuma the warrior. What is he doing seated beside lesser people? Where is his leopard skin? And all these strangers: hunters from Chivi, a warrior from Chivi, a Majira warrior, other Majira, some Dziva Hungwe and finally most are Dhuma's own people: elders and headmen. But who is that porcine commoner with the big stomach actually seated beside the chief? He looks like a court jester of some sort. Strange that many different clans of the king should be in one place. Ah, here is the reason: three no-knees are seated among the warriors and hunters at a table: another abomination of the no-knees.

As the ancestral bird soared down for a closer look, it became suddenly entangled in a cloth cage. Black, red, yellow and green bars hemmed in the bird and it was dismayed. But the men rose and doffed their hats to it and the women crossed their arms to it.

Miss Felicity Mandebvu, the choir mistress, shushed the already silent girls, smart but twitchy in their sharply pressed light blue blouses and navy skirts and the equally quiet boys in their khaki shirts and black trousers. These celestial voices were scheduled to lead the assembly in the singing of the national anthem. Behind the table, covered by a sharply pressed embroidered white cloth, stood the headmaster of Chose trying to hold in his stomach and suppressing the urge to push up his spectacles. Also gracing the table with their presence were the District Administrator, who quit girdling his gut two years ago and the Member of Parliament, being a thin man, didn't have a bulge to hold in. Mr. Makumbe, ZANU PF branch chairman, tried to hold back a sneeze. Chief Dhuma, in a new brown suit, fingered a vial of snuff in his jacket pocket and finally Mathias Van der Merwe, bursting in his tan safari suit, patriotically held his hat against his chest. The less important teachers cluttered up the back rows behind the table.

When the eagle was half way up the pole, Miss Mandebvu gave the signal and the choir bloomed into song. It was *Ishe Komborera Afrika* (God Bless Africa). After the choir asked the ancestors to protect them . . .

"Ba ah ah ah ah Bah!" A coarse bleating accompanied the singers. The choir resumed only to be again harmonized by ". . . Baaaaaaaaaaaaaaaa!" The saboteurs were insistent. Subversive smiles creased the corners of many mouths, including the six openings at the high table.

Answering the summons for God and the ancestors to come and give Africa their blessing, five ruminant

234

representatives of the spirit world strolled to the table and boldly eyed the defenceless bougainvillea blooms. Then they brazenly began to feast on the delicate pink blossoms. Thanks to decorum, the chef could only gawk helplessly. The finale was also accompanied by "Baaaaaaaaaaa -aaaaaaaaaaaaa!" with a satisfying belch ending the song. Courtesy of three black and two tawny goats, even the MP and the DA couldn't keep straight faces. Meanwhile the backbone of Chose was in convulsions. There hadn't been such a sustained performance of humour since Manasseh Chidhuma farted in the first staff meeting in 1984, a year and a half ago. As then, now the headmaster wiped his eyes, replaced his spectacles and loudly cleared his throat to restore order and proper solemnity to the occasion.

"Baaaaaaaaaaaaaaaaa........"

Exasperated Chef Urozvi shouted. "Mr. Boarding Master, get rid of these bloody *budzis*!"

Willing volunteers from the ranks of students gleefully threw stones and sticks at the stubborn cud chewers, who dodged and danced around but refused to leave the assembly area. Finally, an older, bearded, form three students managed to get a headlock on the biggest black beast and hauled it off stage. Divide and rule being the most effective remedy, the four other saboteurs clomped after their leader. It seemed obvious that some enterprising lads were going to gorge themselves on juicy goat meant in their subterranean hang out later that night. The owner of the goats would never dare to claim them.

At last the headmaster regained control and began his speech of welcome. The obligatory hierarchical

budzi - goat

235

introductions prefaced his talk.

"Good afternoon Member of Parliament, the honourable Cde.---, ZANU PF Provincial Secretary, Cde.-------, District Council Chairman and Chairman of the District ZANU PF, Cde.------, ZANU PF Branch Chairman, Cde. Makumbe, Chief Dhuma, Headmasters, Invited Guests, Staff and Students of Chose Secondary School, Comrades and Friends, Gentlemen and Ladies, it is my pleasure this afternoon to open the fifth annual Africa Day celebrations."

A cool film of shade from the msassa trees coated Mathias as he sat back in the student's chair. He succeeded in listening only to the cackling of crows and weavers among the leaves and the frantic bleating of the goats in the distance. He never liked speeches of any kind. But sometimes these monologues, a part of the need to express often unrealized ideals, were necessary to mark a place in time and recall the purpose of existence.

The MP droned on about Zimbabwe's role in the Organization of African Unity and the Commonwealth of Nations and their deliberations on South Africa. The ZANU Provincial Secretary chirruped on educational ties between African countries. At this point the honourable Cde Headmaster Urozvi simmered in futile rage, for the secretary by some devious plot, had stolen his thunder.

Mat noticed the interplay and grinned like a replete lion, actually hoping that nobody was going to cheat him of his painstakingly prepared speech on agricultural improvement in Chisungo District. "That bleeding DA better stick to politics and the training centre," he growled to himself. Then Mat was jolted out of his half trance by Cde. Makumbe as he roused the audience out of its torpor with the usual slogans against laziness and sugar daddies. Now Mat was able to go over the main points of his speech.

Instead, he thought *back to the first devastating and giddy experience in Debbie Goerzen's house. Was that only a little over a year ago? God, time played tricks-- so few months but so many changes.* Yet their passage was painfully slow and arduous.

Mathias felt like a man squinting into the steely dawn at his rows and rows of maize which had to be weeded or else. And there was the back-straining toil, plant by plant, weed by weed, plucking and churning the soil again. Into the morning hours, sweat sparkling on bare back, thighs and calves straining: the occasional rest and to work again. Afternoon's sizzling sun slowing down the pace but the man cannot relent. And finally, the last row greenly wavered in the weary farmer's gaze. At last the final weed and the last churning of earth under a darkening sky: a sense of accomplishment, a well-earned rest knowing full well that another weedy field awaited him on the other side of night. This was the law of the universe: nothing was ever constant except for the effort to adapt and survive. The headmaster's voice cut into Matty's thoughts.

"And now Comrades and Friends, it gives me great pleasure to introduce you to - well most of us know Cde. Mathias Van der Merwe, locally known as Murimi we Mombe. His family has lived in Chisungo District for four generations. I am delighted that Murimi has graciously consented to give us his expert advice on farming. And this to me, and I am sure that all you will agree, is a fine example of what reconciliation means to develop and maintain a stronger and more peaceful Zimbabwe."

Cheers, whistles and ululations supported the chef's inspired introduction of the well-liked Boer. Mat stood firmly and unafraid, no longer assailed by a dead voice. He approached the microphone with expectancy and pleasure.

He was freed.

THE END

Glossary

All words are from Shona, Karanga dialect, unless otherwise stated.

ambuya - grandmother, or a respectful address to an older woman.

amai - mother, formal use - see *mai*

baba - father, or a respectful address to an adult male. Usage - Baba Tavonga - father of Tavonga

babalazi - hangover

blas - bottle store Shonglish (Shona English) – buddy, friend see *shamwari*

bodo – no, negative in ChiKaranga standard Shona - aiwa

chef – origin unknown –used to indicate an African government official or one's supervisor or a general term for the social and political elite. Often used humorously and derisively.

chi - diminutive prefix - usage chimuti - little tree

chibuku - opaque beer made from rapoko and maize which was commercially sold under the same name.

Chilapalapa - is a simplified argot of Zulu some English and Afrikaans. This language was formed in the mines of South Africa and is used in workplace situations where several language groups must communicate. In Zimbabwe, it was and is considered insulting to be spoken to in this language away from the job because it was used to ridicule Africans and their languages. See

Wrex Tarr comedian specializing in Chilapalapa.

chisi - the Sabbath, day of rest according to the traditional lunar calendar. The specific day depends on the area and totem of the people. In Dhuma's village chisi was on Wednesdays. On this day, the chief holds his court and beer is brewed for the ancestors.

doro – beer

doro re ChiKaranga – home brew or seven days mostly made from rapoko, about 10% alcohol

futsek (futseki)- (Afrikaans (woertsek) now Shonalized) - a curse - go away. Standard Shona expression is *ivapo*.

gomeh - a special word to announce a beer drink.

humwe - a purely Karanga word only used in the rural areas of Masvingo province. This is a traditional celebration usually taking place on the Sabbath where *doro re ChiKaranga*, seven-day home brew, is consumed and the ancestors are contacted. See *ndare*. Only women past child bearing age are allowed to brew this beer. Young fertile women are not ritually pure. Ritual purity had more to do with the conflict between sexual (profane) and spiritual (sacred) energy.

infana – little brother – term of endearment for a younger friend or social subordinate.

imba yanopiro - a round mud house specifically used to talk to the family ancestors. However, many ceremonies are either held in the doorway or at the grave of the ancestors if weather permits.

iwe - informal you - used in the same way as thou: usually an address to close friends, subordinates or younger people. It is considered a grave insult to address an older person as iwe. The correct address to an elder or an adult is *imi*. When Chigwede called Mathias iwe in Chapter 14, the policeman wanted to degrade the farmer.

ivapo - curse - go away - see futsek

jong (Afrikaans) - boy, kid. Often used as a term of derision for a black in South Africa during apartheid.

jongwe - rooster, cock. Incidentally, this is the party emblem of ZANU PF, the ruling party who are mainly connected to the Shona population.

kaffir - (Afrikaans) - from the Arabic kafir meaning infidel or unbeliever. Kaffir was and still is in some circles a common term of derision for an African.

kaffirboetie - (Afrikaans) - literally means the little brother of the African. This term is used to describe a white person who sides with the blacks.

kraal - (Afrikaans) - either an enclosure used to house animals or the smallest Zimbabwean political unit composed of several often-related households. It was a term of derision used by some Europeans to denote an African's traditional home.

laager (Afrikaans) - circle of wagons used by the Boers for defence during the Zulu Wars, the Great Trek of the 1830s and 1840s and the Boer War 1900. Up till 1990 it was used as a metaphor for apartheid.

maborn - a term of derision used for an African town dweller. Blacks in Zimbabwe say that no African comes from town because everybody's ancestors are buried in the rural areas. Also, every African has a home or is at least a connected to a plot of land in the communal areas. Mr. Jeans, the town man in Chapter 12, is completely alienated from his roots in Chisungo District.

macomrade - (Shonglish)- comrades, plural. See comrade.

mai - mom, familiar - can also be a respectful address for an adult female. Usage - Mai Nyasha - mother of Nyasha.

mai we- an exclamation, oh ma- a lot like 'oh my God'.

mopane - a common straight holed deciduous tree with termite resistant wood.

msassa - deciduous tree whose leaves turn red in the spring (Oct. – Dec.).

mubunu or *mbunu*- boer, Afrikaner, or a general word meaning any white racist. Plural *mabunu* - boers

mugwagawa - a pure Karanga word - road, highway.

mujiba plural *majiba* - children who acted as spies, messengers and gun runners for the comrades.

munt - (Rhodesian dialect probably from Afrikaans) a term of derision for an African.

murimi - farmer - from the verb *kurima* - to till land.

murungu - white person - *marungu* - plural, white people. Another term for the whites is no-knees. When the British South Africa Company soldiers first came into Shona country, the people looked at their trousers and couldn't see their knees. Often no-knees is a term of derision.

musha – an African's home village where his/her ancestors are buried.

mutengesi – *matengesi* –plural - traitor, sell out - from the verb *kutengesa* to sell.

muti - medicine or tree

n'anga- a healer, herbalist

ndare - beer drink, see humwe

ngozi - an avenging spirit

ningi - a low despicable person, a thing, nothing. Also, a Rhodesian term of derision for an African.

nya (Afrikaans) - no, negative

nyimo – monkey orange – an indigenous dark orange fruit inside a husk which is gathered in the bush. It tastes like a peach or a mango depending on its ripeness.

oom – uncle (Afrikaans)

oopa - grandfather (Afrikaans)

pamusoroi – excuse me

povo - (Portuguese from the Mozambican War of Independence ending in 1975) - adults who helped the ZANLA guerrillas as spies, gun runners, and procurement officers.

pungwe - a secret night meeting held by comrades where the masses were politicized. Post- independence usage - an all- night party.

rapoko - (South African English probably from Zulu, now has common usage in Shona and English) - this is a small brown grain that grows on tassels. It is reasonably drought resistant. It appears to be in the same family as West African guinea corn. The porridge made from rapoko is deep brown and is a delicious alternative to maize porridge, especially with pumpkin leaves in groundnut sauce called *mrewa ne dovi*. The beer made from rapoko is tingly and potent, about 10 per cent alcohol by volume known as the doro re ChiKaranga (Karanga beer).

rora – bride price – unlike European tradition where the woman brings the dowry, the Shona bridegroom gives gifts and a portion of his wealth to the bride's family, usually in the form of cows from his kraal. Even educated, middle class, professional men will walk the nine or ten cows from his village to her village to prove his strength and integrity.

saka - therefore

sadza - a stiff maize porridge eaten with meat, vegetables or milk. Sadza is the main staple like potatoes and bread are in the West.

sekuru- uncle or grandfather: a term of respect for an old man or for your social superior.

sissy (Shonglish) - sister, or female friend.

sandawana – evil magic, ritual dismembering of a corpse or even a living person for witchcraft.

shanwari - friend, comrade

shanwari yapamoyo – friend of the heart – bosom buddy

svikiro - spirit medium, a trained religious person who contacts the ancestors through a trance. There is usually one or two *masvikiro* (plural) in every village. Both men and women can become spirit mediums based on their spiritual awareness rather than gender or class. They always attend the village humwe. Both male and female spirit mediums, though allowed to marry, sometimes choose celibacy.

tumbu - stomach

va - mister

vakomana brothers, boys - a term of endearment used by the people for the ZANLA fighters or comrades.

VaPenga – insane people

verechte – (Afrikaans) – proper, righteous

Zinatha – Zimbabwean National Traditional Healers' Association: After Independence, the government formally recognized traditional n'anga - herbalists and svikiro - spirit mediums as legal practitioners of medicine and psychiatry.

Terms of Derision used by Rhodesians to indicate Africans: Af, baboon, bobojaan, gandanga, gorilla, hout, kaffir, monkey, munt, ningi, picanin, sadza, terr.

Terms Of derision used by Africans to indicate a white supremacist: mubunu, no-knees, or a range of predators like leopard, hyena, etc.